AMERICAN
MONEY
PUBLISHING

WE PUBLISH THE REALIST BOOKS

American Money Publishing, LLC

Donald J. Trump: The New Hitler

Copyright © 2018 by Genaro Patterson

ISBN: 9781729350430

Printed in the United States of America

genaro.patterson.hfo@gmail.com

Acknowledgments

I wish there were a lot of people I could thank, but unfortunately there's not. However, I would like to thank everyone who constantly reminded me of my faults and failures and never acknowledged my accomplishments. I just want you to know I feed off of your negative energy. No matter how hard the world hits me, I'll get back up. No one is perfect. We've all made bad decisions. Yet, they tell me what I could've been and should've been as if they've never made any mistakes.

I've even been told I was cursed; and since I've been cursed I've cursed my mother. But I could never believe that. I believe a certain amount of suffering comes before success. I've suffered more than most, but I refuse to let it beat me. I believe everyone is in control of their destiny and although I haven't controlled mine the way I should have, it's not over yet. Therefore, no matter my situation or circumstances, I still try to make my tomorrows better than my yesterdays. So, thank you. Without you there would be no me.

DONALD J. TRUMP: THE NEW HITLER

Written By

Patterson

DONALD J. TRUMP: THE NEW HITLER

MAKE AMERICA **HATE** AGAIN

"I COULD STAND IN THE MIDDLE OF FIFTH AVENUE AND SHOOT SOMEBODY AND I WOULDN'T LOSE ANY VOTES."

— DONALD J. TRUMP

Prologue

The New Hitler

"*Not my President! Not my President! Not my President!*" people in the United States chanted as they marched through their cities and states, realizing just who they had elected for their President. He was now the most powerful man in the world. "*I will build a wall so big and so strong the Mexicans will never be able to get over it and I will send every one of them back that are here!*" Trump told the world. Whites have started hating blacks again and they abhor Mexicans. Hate crimes are rising at an alarming rate and mixed children are confused. Little boys and girls would cry, wondering what will happen to them and their parents. David Duke, the leader of the Ku Klux Klan, would tweet, "*Today is a great day for white people. White power to all white people!*"

The people would gather in front of Trump Tower and hold up signs that would say, "THE NEW

HITLER" while chanting *"Not my President!"* Trump would even add Steve Bannon to his administration as possible Chief Strategist. He's a master of political theater and a champion of white supremacy. The country would be in an uproar, sad and confused about how the billionaire real estate mogul won the election by a landslide in the Electoral College. The people would live in fear, not knowing what to expect from the man they called racist, sexist, unsavory and just plain evil. r

"*I love war!*" he would scream to the people. "*I'll do anything to women, even grab them by the pussy!*" he would say with no shame or respect. But that was just the tip of the iceberg that added insult to injury. It was the fear of the unknown; fear of what the newly elected President would do next that had the country on edge. The world was being introduced to the new "Hitler."

"Men have never been good; they are not good; they never will be."
— *Karl Barth*

Donald J. Trump

DONALD J. TRUMP. What will he do?
What won't he do?

Chapter One

Enemy Within

America has its enemies, but sometimes it seems as if though the enemy was within America itself. Sometimes a person or people can become a risk to their country. Because of our history of white/black racism, it's not abnormal that a powerful white man can emerge with new and different ideas that differ from the majority of the people. His ideas could move in a different direction from the current direction of the country but could still appeal to a lot of people who felt the same way as he did. Therefore, the risk could come from within America's own party.

This man talks about putting the country first. He talks about not wasting money protecting other countries. And he talks about cutting taxes — the largest tax cut since Reagan. He advocates building a wall to keep all the immigrants out and deporting up to three million of them out of the country. He wants to implement extreme vetting, free and fair trade and bring education back to the States. Republican Senator Howard Baker, who is no stranger to making corrections within the party, is a memory from the Watergate scandal for showing the power-abusing United States President Richard Nixon the door. Plus, Democratic President Franklin D. Roosevelt's (FDR) own Vice President, John Nance Garner, is remembered for standing tall against FDR's plan to pack the Supreme Court.

With the rise of Trump, the GOP leaders must choose how they want to be remembered. The new masseur who speaks what so many want to hear is being confronted with many unsavory actions which includes an audio tape of the Presidential nominee bragging about attempted adultery and sexual assault which caused dozens of Republican leaders to abandon him. One of those leaders was John McCain whom he also told, "I don't like people who get caught. I'm a winner. I like people who win (referring to McCain's time as a Prisoner of War)." But he wasn't alone. Other senators and governors from across the country would also distance themselves from this man.

A "USA Today" network survey showed that 26% of Republican governors and members refused to endorse Trump because of his mindset, but what about the other 74%? He's attacked Hispanics and Muslims, and a decades-long record of contempt for women. He has a long list of lawsuits for stiffing small businesses, a list of bankruptcies and a tendency to brag about the size of his manhood. It was as if it didn't matter what he did or what was revealed, the real estate mogul would still have most of the senior leaders to remain by his side as he fought to become the next President. And although the Speaker of the House, Paul Ryan, would make attempts to denounce the infamous Trump for his sickening words, he did not withdraw his endorsement. Trump was already a billionaire who was very powerful and it was like he knew he couldn't or wouldn't lose, no matter what he did. He once said, "I can stand in the middle of Fifth Avenue and shoot somebody and I wouldn't lose any votes." That's how confident he was. Trump believes he is a winner who never loses.

Rise of a Mogul

His rise to the top has been extraordinary and one of exceptional privilege with the best of opportunities that presented themselves. Before the world knew Donald Trump, he was born in Queens, New York to Fred and Mary Trump. Fortunately for Trump, his father was a real estate developer who made millions from adding garages to previously constructed homes. He was the fourth of five children but it didn't take long for his father to realize that Trump had the "gift." He, just like his father, gained an interest in real estate. But it wasn't in residential property. His vision would come later.

He would attend the Ivy League Wharton School of Business where he sharpened his skills toward becoming an entrepreneur. Although the country was at war, he was able to dodge the Vietnam draft not once, but five times during the 60's and 70's. This was done solely to allow him to finish his education without interruption. In school he would realize that he was different than the other students, having a bigger vision of what he wanted to be and what he wanted to become. But even though he was away at school, he and his father had cemented a good relationship.

By the time of his graduation, he already knew what he wanted to do in life. He wanted to follow in his father's footsteps. But because he dreamed big and envisioned bigger, he saw big buildings in his future. As a result, after graduating, he asked his father for a one million dollar loan. After laying out his plan as to how he would use the money, his father happily agreed. So he set sights on Manhattan in New York where the real estate was not doing so well. He had found and located a huge building in serious need of repair and his vision was to refurbish and turn it into a high rise hotel. Everyone he talked to said it couldn't be done; that it would be a huge mistake; and that it was also in a terrible location. But Trump had a vision and a dream and he was not going to let anyone or anything stop him from making them come true.

He had the vision and the drive and all he needed was for the bank to loan him the rest of the money to make it all become a reality. But when he solicited the banks he hit a snag. They all said he had no real estate experience and decided not to loan him the money. It was a serious disappointment but it didn't stop Donald. He simply found someone who did have real estate experience and was able to seal the deal. Trump would then start work on his vision, hiring undocumented immigrant workers so that he could begin construction immediately. Any problem that would emerge, he would solve it. He had an attitude of "no problems, only solutions." His proud father watched closely as his son made bigger-than-life decisions on his very first project. Donald believed: Think big and big things will happen.

After months and months of construction (and using cheap steel) Trump's incredible high rise skyscraper was complete. It was a masterpiece. Trump became a real estate mastermind overnight and an instant millionaire. He was the talk of New York. He increased property values and the media called him "brilliant." He was also a man who paid close attention to details. "When my siblings and I started out, my father had us work alongside project bosses and job foremen to learn the dignity of work," Donald Trump said. Donald Trump eventually took control of Trump Management, the multi-million dollar family business. He would later rename the business, The Trump Organization.

"Gently guide fortune and help determine the future by thinking ahead."
— *Robert Greene*

American   Money   Publishing

WE PUBLISH THE REALIST BOOKS

Chapter Two

Underestimated

Trump has always been into himself and has relished in his accomplishments. He believes he is a winner and does not believe in losing. Whenever anyone enters his office in his New York Trump Tower, and wherever their eyes would fall, there are wall-to-wall images of the business tycoon. The walls are plastered with "Playboy," "GQ," "People," "Newsweek," and "Rolling Stone" magazines plus many more. There are piles of literature for his campaign, "MAKE AMERICA GREAT AGAIN." However, for America to be great again meant whites would need to be recognized as the supreme race again. There were also stacks of recent Trump-fronted publications on a desk so packed that it resembled a dentist's office waiting room as well as a mound of Trump-covered copies of "The Economist."

The pride Trump takes in such self-aggrandizing "Trumpery" is almost touching but it's also narcissistic. His Aladdin's cave of celebrity puff doubles as his headquarters on the 26th floor and is sufficiently eccentric to recall why his announcement of his candidacy was at first laughable and ridiculed. He seemed slightly retarded and uneducated when he spoke. It appeared as if he was more respected as the real estate billionaire Trump. But after hearing him speak, he made America wonder how he made all that money. He looked like a reality TV star without an ounce of political experience. He has been challenged on issues and has changed his political stripes at least four times. But nothing he does appears to hurt him. His flaws and mistakes seem to only make him stronger.

In May, 2016, Trump would prove to the world that he was a serious contender in the race to become President of the United States. He would be victorious in Indiana which resulted in him being made the presumptive Republican nominee. His other remaining opponents would realize their defeat and drop out of the race. This would include respected prominent men like Governor John Kasich and Senator Ted Cruz. The world had underestimated Trump by not realizing the country was divided and felt the same way as Trump. He failed to take advice from anybody; the world couldn't see his vision and believed the man was crazy. However, the same must not be said of the threat his egomania and damaging nativism represents to America and the world.

His success in becoming the elected President was based on his engaged view of America being extremely dark and widely acceptable to outsiders who are un-American. He had tapped into something the Democrats missed as well as the rest of the world. Two-thirds of Americans believed the economy was rigged in favor of the rich. Statistics found that seven out of ten Americans felt their politicians did not care about them and would just make promises to get elected. For decades, minimum wages have remained under $10.00 an hour and the prices of food and real estate continued to climb. Much of the work environment declined due to struggling to adapt to falling demand for low-skilled factory labor which took a hard hit. Plus, it was true that America's infrastructure was crumbling. And

America's Middle Eastern policy had seen wars raged across the region. Terrorism was threatening the lives of Americans and people began to fear living a normal life without fear of being attacked in some type of violent way.

But for most of the Republican race, Mr. Trump would only receive 35% of the vote and it appeared those votes were mainly cast by white, uneducated men who didn't receive an education further than high school. With those type of numbers he was considered a weak front-runner and likely not to win a majority in any state. It looked like Trump would get "trumped" out after the field was separated with him at a disadvantage when his opponents split the mainstream Republican vote. But again, Trump would prove everybody wrong. He would win the majority outright in his home state of New York. He would repeat that feat six times on the trot; in Indiana he would win 53% of the vote.

When the world saw this, Trump would pick up support from other groups which were surprisingly women who once detested him, and college students who were once opposed to him. For some odd and unknown reason Evangelical Christians were always magnetically drawn to him. It was the working-class Evangelicals in particular who took Trump to victory in the southern states like South Carolina and Georgia. In Indiana he won over Evangelicals who represented half the state's primary electorate by eight percentage points, although he had been married three times and didn't appear religious. That wasn't expected at all.

But Trump would continue to engage in the unexpected with his opponents through more verbal assaults. He would slander Ted Cruz's father, a well-known Evangelical preacher, without any evidence at all. He suggested that Cruz's father had played a part in the assassination of John F. Kennedy: "I mean, what was he doing? What was he doing with Lee Harvey Oswald shortly before the death of Kennedy? Before the shooting? It's horrible." Surprisingly, to the world, Donald Trump was on the verge of breaking the record for voters who voted in Republican primaries and won. With his attraction to riled activists and a growing population, the growing breadth of his appeal, and the fact that despite his divisiveness, Trump had a solid chance to become the next President of the United Sates.

Donald J. Trump wants what all men want: "THEY WANT MORE." History remembers dictators, kings and presidents. Although they do remember celebrities, there's no comparison to how they remember presidents. As president, if he does anything memorable, his name will be remembered for thousands of years.

The little boy in the movie "Troy" told Brad Pitt, "He's big, real big. I wouldn't fight 'em."

Brad Pitt responded, "That's why they will never remember your name."

Men want to be remembered. They want to leave their mark on this earth. These are the men who are extraordinary, not ordinary. No matter what, Donald J. Trump will make himself memorable. He has no limit. He will go where no man has gone. He knows he can't satisfy all men, that is why he will only please himself. He's fearless, smart and still hungry. He thirsts for the ultimate in power because all he's ever known is power.

"Nothing is built on stone; all is built on sand,
but we must build as if the sand is stone."
— Jorge Luis Burges

American Money Publishing

WE PUBLISH THE REALIST BOOKS

Hillary Rodham Clinton

AMP

American   Money   Publishing

WE PUBLISH THE REALIST BOOKS

Chapter Three

Hillary

If Trump's opponent had been anybody other than Hillary Clinton, it's a strong possibility that the real estate mogul wouldn't have won the presidency. His odds were enhanced by having an opponent that the world also disliked. The FBI was investigating her because of possible classified emails on her private email server. But after dismissing the investigation, surprisingly, the FBI reopened it in the last few weeks of the election. The media labeled her a liar and over half the voters had a poor view of her. She would win the more popular vote but in the end it would not be enough.

Hillary (and most people) believed she would basically beat out Trump because his views were unpopular with the views of the people whom she had won against in all but two of the 58 head-to-head polls. However, such polling can sometimes become poor predictions if prior to the party conventions which are held to focus voter's minds on their party's agenda. Being an unpopular candidate is always a weakness. Therefore, Clinton felt very confident that she would be victorious.

The general election would prove to be ugly with Clinton and Trump attacking one another viciously. There appeared to be little probing of Trump moderating his positions. His positions were mostly extreme to be credibly revised. Apparently he felt exonerated by his success in the primaries and Trump had little interest in changing his tactics which were aggressive with often offensive methods he used with anyone or anything he disliked; and at the moment he disliked Hillary. "She's playing the woman card. That's all she's got going. She's got nothing else going. The only thing she's got is the woman card. And she plays it to the hilt," barked Trump who at that time was not liked by 70% of American women.

But Trump didn't care. He was running an unconventional campaign that had never been done before. He wasn't kissing anybody's ass and he vowed not to be bought-off by anybody. Although, he made claims that Hillary could be bought. "Such a nasty woman," Trump calls Hillary. "If Hillary Clinton was a man I don't think she would get 5% of the vote," Trump shouted to his crowd of supporters. "Don't you think a man who has this type of economic genius is a lot better for the United States than a woman?" Rudy Giuliani shouted to Trump supporters at a Trump rally. "She is crooked Hillary," Trump would call her as his supporters clapped and cheered   But Clinton maintained a double-digit lead among college-educated women and a significant lead with suburban women.

Then an "Access Hollywood" videotape recording from 2005 was discovered. The tape recorded Trump bragging about how he "does" women. "I can do anything to women; even grab 'em by the pussy." Debate moderator, Anderson Cooper, asked him about it, explaining his behavior was considered sexual assault. "It's just locker room talk," Trump said. But then more women started coming out and accusing him of the exact same things he had boasted about. When the tape was made public many Republicans started to jump ship. They had reached their breaking point. Paul Ryan, The Speaker of the House, encouraged down-ballot candidates to cut all ties with Trump.

The tapes hurt Trump because 60% of all white women felt it was a big deal. But Trump also had white women voters who felt it would not affect their vote. "Lewd language and sexual misconduct had nothing to do with my vote," Dorothy Baskin said. "I don't care about Trump's locker room talk. I talked to my husband and asked, 'be honest with me, do men talk like this?' He said, 'of course, Dorothy'." That was all she needed to hear. But other women said Trump had no sense of decency. However, Trump believed he could still win without support from women, African-Americans, Hispanics, Muslims, immigrants, or the LGBT community. He knew that as long as he had white voters who believed that being white was the ultimate race, he knew he could win.

He made the world believe in him and hate all those who stood in his way which included Hillary Clinton. He also pointed out to blacks that it was Bill Clinton and Senator Joe Biden who authored a devastating crime bill that Hillary Clinton supported and stated, "Young black men are super predators." They finally admitted the war on drugs was really a war on blacks. That law crippled the black community, creating mass incarcerations of blacks with a minimum of ten years and more. The law destroyed families, took fathers away by the thousands. It was a new era of hi-tech slavery which is still felt today. It is the most diabolical and egregious law ever known to man. Its focus was to depopulate the black community and have them work in prison for 12 cents an hour for 85% of their sentence. It was the starter flame for the "three strikes you're out" law and its outrageous prison enhancements. It was that law which made black people not trust Hillary Clinton or her husband Bill Clinton. (This ultimately caused Hillary to lose the election).

I Know the Game

"I know the game better than anyone," Trump would proudly tell his supporters. "I've been on the other side.' He was believable and convincing. He was exposing how politicians are greedy, money-hungry and don't care about the people. He let the world know that he had been on both sides; he had played the game and as a candidate for president, he would not be like them because he was not one of them. "I am not a politician," he would say. "Nobody can pay me off." Everybody knew Donald Trump was a billionaire so they knew he didn't need money.   Therefore, again, his statement was believable.

Donald Trump was selling America a dream and promising to take them out of their living nightmare. When he talked about blacks, he said, "They're just being used by the damn politicians." As was everybody else who lied to voters to get elected. Trump was pulling out all the stops. He believed that if he did lose, he didn't want to go down in history for getting blown out. Most politicians who run for president for the first time usually don't win, especially against a seasoned veteran like Hillary Clinton. But Trump hammered home to the people that politicians were corrupt and could not be trusted to do the right thing.   He told them politicians would make a lot of promises and after they won they would only do what was best for them. Plus, the people knew that was true from past elections. It was Donald's plan to demolish the 162 year political organization that the world had become accustomed to.   The brash, boastful billionaire real estate mogul—driven by money, power and fame—had convinced his supporters that he had nothing to gain and that he only wanted to help them. But what they didn't know was: It was all just a façade.

Trump

A foreigner driving through the streets of New York might believe Trump owned the entire state. It's not abnormal to see his name in larger-than-life letters on many larger-than-life skyscrapers and high rise buildings. It wouldn't be farfetched to characterize him as egocentric which many said about Adolph Hitler. Trump's name is on so many buildings that he even allows other building owners to use his name on their buildings—for a price of course. That's how much prestige his name once carried. His name had so much value that he was able to license it. It's as if though this is his world and he is the king.

When you pass by the newspaper and magazine stands it is his face and name which dominates the front pages and front covers. Trump has been on the cover of almost every magazine in circulation, including "Forbes," "People," "Time," "The Economist," "GQ," "Mad," "Rolling Stones," "Entrepreneur," "Weird" and more. Also, there are Trump steaks, Trump sheets, Trump golf courses and a Trump reality show. And, he has Trump Tower, Trump Plaza, Trump Park Avenue and he had the

Trump Taj Mahal. Plus, there are all the other buildings which display the name of Trump.

Everything is judged by its appearance. Trump is a master at knowing that what's not seen counts for nothing. His face is on every cover; he is talked about on Fox News and CNN damn near every day. Donald Trump *is* news. Everything he does is news, including his views on Vladimir Putin, the President of Russia. Trump never allows himself to get lost in the crowd of this world. He refuses to be buried in oblivion. If it's not Trump himself out front, then it will be one of his larger-than-life buildings. As President of the United States, he now has world leaders worried and talking about him daily. They're wondering if he will pull out of the Paris Agreement and no longer honor the Paris climate pact.

Trump tries to be conspicuous at all costs. He has made himself a magnet for attention and as a result he has created an image the world sees as bigger than life. He is rich, powerful, confusing, egocentric and mysterious and no one is exactly sure how he thinks. He has no fear, no shame and no respect. He will not hesitate to fight or destroy his enemy or anyone he believes is potentially an enemy. Trump is not like the timid masses; he is Trump and you would've had to be living in a cave, without any technology, not to know about him. His image is unforgettable and his ways are controversial. He's been named in scandals and paid out settlements of $25 million dollars after saying, "I'll never settle." His homes and hotels are adorned with gold furniture and trimmings. His office sits on the 26th floor of Trump Tower with the best view in New York as he looks down on everyone and professes, "I like war," keeping his enemies in fear. He shines brighter than everyone around him. His notoriety has helped to bring him power and it doesn't matter if he is being praised, slandered or attacked, Donald J. Trump is never ignored.

"Court attention at all cost" — Law #6

— Robert Greene

AMP

American   Money   Publishing

WE PUBLISH THE REALIST BOOKS

Chapter Four

Ranting

"TRUMP! TRUMP! TRUMP!" shouted the predominantly all-white crowd. Trump's rallies were consistently looking like biker meetings. "It's really a special place for me," Trump said about Manchester, New York. "This is where I won my first victory!" he shouts with glee to the crowd. He feels comfortable; he is speaking to the people who want what he wants to see—America white again. "Over the next 47 days we are all going to work hard to win this state..." He doesn't tell them what he will do to make America great again; instead, he quickly changes his script and starts to talk about his favorite subject: himself. "If I didn't win here, who knows where I'd be," he said while smiling. "Maybe I'd be building buildings or something." He brags about his business acumen and the audience loves it as they roar with joy. That is the Trump they fell in love with; this man full of confidence; a self-congratulating egocentric who ramrodded his way to the Republican nomination.

Trump is known for doing it his way with unscripted rants that were music to the ears of students who had never taken a test without studying. He was the script-less wonder that refused to listen to advice from people who were smarter than him. "Hillary Clinton only believes in government by and for the powerful!" Then he started ranting about "crooked Hillary." He speaks harshly and abusively as he convinces his supporters she is no good. It is confusing as he rants about several Clinton controversies in disreputable language. He berated Bill Clinton for the speaking fees paid to him by companies like the Swedish telecom giant Ericsson while it had business before Hillary's State Department. He even used the phrase, "The exemption of telecom giant Ericsson."

He criticized moves to give foundation donors disputable reconstruction contracts in Haiti, and a seat on an intelligence advisory board. "Hillary ran the State Department as if it was her own personal hedge fund," he told his newfound followers.

Although it made no sense, not even to people who hate hedge fund managers, he mentions another controversy. He brought up an issue involving a Russian uranium company. Then he brought up an issue involving The Swiss Bank UBS. It was obvious he was rambling. He couldn't remember the last five things he'd talked about in his speech.   Even more revealing is his dismount, "But these examples are only the tip of the Clinton-corruption iceberg!" he continued. The bottom line is Trump would say anything to discredit and denigrate Hillary.

Adolph Hitler

Smith's accurate observations about the growing power of Hitler (here in 1934) and the German military led to accusations that he was pro-German.

Just Like Hitler

Adolph Hitler was a German dictator whose unlikely rise in power allowed him to become the most powerful man in Germany. He rose to power during a time when economic anxiety was high, the government was polarized and gridlocked, and elites were being subjected to rising resentment. Stepping in to fill this void was Adolph Hitler. After he was in power he divided Germany with hate and confusion. He was dismissed by a major magazine's editor as "a big mouth and pathetic dunderhead." But Hitler knew how to play a crowd and fan fear and anger. Then he would offer himself as the strongman needed to shake things up. He was charming in company but never forgot an insult. He was resentful of intellectuals and could not bear public humiliation.

Adolph Hitler was a man with a recognizable past. The world remembers him as a man responsible for mass murders and a reign of terror. In 2017 his name could easily be Donald Trump. Both seemed to share a lot of the same characteristics. When we talk about Hitler, it's almost as if we're talking about Trump. Trump has a big mouth and is a pathetic dunderhead according to the media. He knows how to play a crowd and uses fear and anger to gain supporters. He presents himself as the person to shake things up and fix it all. He could be charming in company but never forgot an insult. He resents intellectuals and can't stand public humiliation. If anyone says anything negative about Trump, he engages in a Tweeting rampage on social media. And just like Hitler, Trump is now working on his legacy. It is scary but we will have to wait and see what legacy Trump will leave. But more than likely, he will lead our nation into war.

On December 1, 2016, before Trump even moved into the White House, China lodged a formal complaint with the United States following a phone call between Trump and Taiwan's leader. It was rumored that Trump wanted to have some hotels built in Taiwan, although it was a conflict of interest to be President and still run a business. It appeared that Trump had already risked a showdown with China after the call. "China doesn't dictate what American leaders do or don't do," a spokesperson for the Trump administration stated. Trump had already told the world, "I like war!" the same as Hitler. And because America is the strongest country in the world it's likely China doesn't scare Trump.

"A scared man can't win"

— *Patterson*

Chapter Five

Farrakhan Speaks

"Barack Obama. We supported him when he was a community organizer. I had never met him but my Chief of Staff at that time, Brother Leonard F. Muhammad, knew Barack Obama and we backed him with money and with help from the FOI (Fruit of Islam) to get him elected. Barack Obama became a United States Senator. That part of the story I will leave for another time. But he visited me—that's all I will say. Later on, he threw his hat in the ring to become President of the United States. However I, at our Savior's Day Convention in 2008, spoke kind words about my brother. But Hillary Clinton had already said she wanted to be President. She and Barack became locked in a battle when there was a debate on "Meet the Press" with

NBS's star reporter, Tim Russert. Then my name came up.

For all of you who want national and state prominence, sometimes I am the "litmus test" to see if white folk can do anything good for you. And some of you are so weak and cowardly that your desires mean more than the integrity of your character. But each time I forgave my brothers and kept moving forward. Barack did not want to denounce me but Hillary forced him and he gave in and said, 'All right, all right. I renounce Farrakhan. I don't want his support.' I supported him anyway. Some of the followers were a little angry with me because they felt he had dissed me. 'BUT IT'S NOT PERSONAL. WHAT'S THE BIG PICTURE? WHAT'S IN THE BEST INTEREST OF OUR PEOPLE?' I told all of those with me, 'Don't you say anything negative about Barack Obama.'

So at 5 o'clock in the morning, me and my wife went around the corner from the National House and voted for our brother. I was very proud of him. 'THE BIGGEST PICTURE IS THAT I HAVE A PICTURE OF MYSELF AND BARACK TOGETHER.' You never saw it because I would never put it out there to give his enemies what they were looking for to hurt him. But he told me straight up, 'Farrakhan, the black vote in

Chicago made me win Chicago, but it was the down-state vote that made me a U.S. Senator. And I will never do anything that will cause me to lose the down-state vote.' And I said to him, 'My brother, your reality is not mine and we need you where you are. So I will never ask you to do anything that will cause you to lose the down-state vote'—and I never have. He was the "bigger picture..." Now in your small mind and heart you are envious because God allowed Barack Obama to be, right now, the most popular leader. No leader has outshined Barack Obama in the hearts of the people.

I know who I am and I know it was his time. It's mine now. So the "bigger picture" is NOT HILLARY CLINTON. THE BIG PICTURE IS NOT DONALD TRUMP. The "bigger picture" is the black masses of America and the American people whose lives are at stake. So what I know I have to tell; and it's a warning to Hillary Clinton and to Donald Trump; to the Democratic and Republican leaders. I want to share something with you from my teacher. I AM SAYING THIS TO THE GOVERNMENT AND I THINK YOU ALREADY KNOW IT: You are not dealing with "Louis." You are dealing with the Elijah in me and the God and the Mahdi that back me! Take it or leave it."

Study the Platforms of Each Party to See if Either Truly Benefits Black Lives

In his book, *The Fall of America*, study what the Honorable Elijah Muhammad said about "this election." Pay attention to these words spoken nearly 50 years ago in the chapter, The National Election: "The black man of America has been privileged by the slave master's children for the last century to vote for whites for the offices to judge and rule. This freedom to vote made the black man in America feel very dignified and proud of himself. He goes to the polls very happy to vote for a white ruler. Today, he is gradually changing to desire to vote for his own kind for such offices of authority. [Now] we must remember that our vote is strong and powerful only when and where the white man can use it to get in the office over his white opponent. [But] after the election and the victory there are very few favors that come from his office to the black voters who helped and aided him in getting in the office."

He continues, "Why [is he like this]? Because he does not [feel he owes] the black voter anything as long as he has to feed, clothe and shelter him."

Mr. Muhammad said, "The black vote could be cast or not cast. The white citizens of the government are going to win and continue to rule [over blacks] anyway..." The talk that's out there right now among the blacks is, "Lord, who's gonna get in? Who's gonna get the honey?" But Elijah Muhammad asked a very good question. He asked, "How much good have the two parties (Republican and Democrat) done for blacks for the last century in the way of freedom, justice and equality" Regardless of what party wins, the die is always set against blacks in America. Injustice, crooked politics and the breeding of corruption under politics have been practiced ever since Adam until the present day rulers. Adam was the first crook. Muhammad writes, "There has not been justice for the black man in this race of people, and this is why their race suffers from the effect of chaos today." He wrote those words 50 years ago for today.

Now what is "chaos?" It is "a state of utter confusion or disorder; a total lack of organization or order; any confused, disorderly mass." Isn't that what we are seeing and hearing everyday concerning the national election? Muhammad says, "There are black politicians who would like to use their black people for selfish greed and will throw them behind any crook with money. Black politicians of this type have sold their black brothers to suffering shame for self-elevation with the crook." I had the flier, "If Satan cast out Satan, he is divided against himself—how then can his kingdom stand?" Hillary and Trump are not the real Satan. Satan is a liar; and they do that, too. But they are low on the totem pole. They are actors in a scheme.

THE SLAVES, OR "A FOOLISH PEOPLE" as we were referred to by Moses, are vexing the slave master. He is very upset with you! "How dare you! How dare you come into my gymnasium that I built for you to show off your prowess in the world of sport and play? And now you're going to take a knee? And sing my national anthem? How dare you pull back your shirt and show that 'Black Lives Matter!' How dare you..." But brother and sister, the truth is, he hates the fact that blacks are coming to realize how much black lives matter. So he will send out Negroes to say, "All lives matter." We have always known that white lives matter when they would kill a black for walking on a sidewalk, or not tipping our hat, or not saying "yassah," or not obeying them, or challenging them on the bottom line of what we worked and earned money for. All lives matter...

But it is black life which is being torn asunder under a genocidal plot. Now, we must say that our lives matter and we must mean it to the point that when people want our vote, we look at them. I am not talking about how it matters to you if they offer you money; how you sacrifice your integrity on the altar of profit to lead your people into their clutches. They have never given blacks what they promised them. And if you study the platform of the Democratic Party, how much of it is real regarding what they plan to do for the masses of black people? They say, "Well listen, we're going to fix the educational system." How are they going to fix it? How can they "fix" an educational system rooted in white supremacy and has been bad for blacks and now bad for them? Or they will say, "Well, we're going to try and get reform in the Justice Department." That's like saying we can reform the devil. How many of us would like to try and reform Satan? How great is your skill at reformation? If we're put in a room with Satan and all that he's taught us, do you think we can reform Satan? My friends are going to vote for Hillary Clinton and I'm not mad at that. They see some value in her because they don't yet know WHO SHE REALLY IS.

"I wake up every morning in a house that
was built by slaves."
— *Michelle Obama*

Unorthodox

Trump, the billionaire real estate mogul, ran the cheapest campaign ever organized in history. He bragged about how he didn't spend any of his money. But he didn't have to. He said so many crazy things that he stayed in the media. Everybody was talking about Trump, including TV shows such as "Saturday Night Live." As his campaign became successful, he started firing. "You're fired," he would say and start recruiting new people he felt could help him win. They tried to get him to try scripted speeches but he continued to refuse. He also decided that even though he used to brag that he didn't need anybody's money, he started accepting money from big spenders who wanted to back him. But he continued his attacks which included a Mexican judge who he said couldn't possibly make the right decision because he was Mexican.

But the world was beginning to understand Trump and knew he would go on politically destructive frenzies. But it was his outrageous, maniacal attacks which caused Donald Trump to explode in the polls. Then he produced another shocker. After constantly telling his supporters he would build a wall and send every illegal immigrant back home, no matter how many families he would split up, he had a sudden change of heart. He told "Fox News," Sean Hannity, that he was considering softening his stance on his immigration controversy. "Everyone agrees we should get the bad ones out, but as I meet and talk with thousands and thousands of people on this subject, they said, "Mr. Trump, I love you. But to take a person that has been here for 15 or 20 years and throw them and their family out, it's so tough, Mr. Trump." The next day he would have his supporters screaming, "Build the wall!" And he promised he would.

"Never make a promise you can't keep."

— Patterson

American   Money   Publishing

WE PUBLISH THE REALIST BOOKS

Chapter Six

Failure

"Great men have big failures," Rudy Giuliani said to "USA Today." He was probably referring to the rise and fall of Donald Trump who endured some vicious personal problems when a scandal exploded in 1989, after Trump shocked the world by becoming a real estate mogul. The scandal erupted after Trump's model mistress, Marla Maples, confronted his lovely wife, Ivana Trump, on the ski slopes of Aspen while he and she were out enjoying themselves. Trump had been secretly dating the beautiful and sexy model. He would have Marla at the Taj Mahal while Ivana was at Trump Towers. The media would get ahold of the story and publicly report in detail the dispute between Marla, Ivana and Donald. It became a media circus when Donald's adultery was revealed. It was a total shock to the world because he and Ivana seemed to be a match made in heaven and an extraordinary team. Ivana was not only a trophy for Trump; she was an exceptional business partner and the mother of three of his children: Donald Jr., daughter Ivanka and Eric.

Trump would eventually divorce Ivana and allow her to walk away with a very generous settlement totaling in the millions of dollars. He called the divorce, "Unpleasant at best." Although he is a man who seems to defy the odds and becomes successful in all that he does, he did find himself in serious money trouble after becoming a billionaire. Amid his personal troubles, he had also acquired major problems with his businesses. It was in the early 90's when the real estate mogul filed for bankruptcy for four of his businesses, including his newest building in Atlantic City which he promised would be a success. He would call it the Trump Taj Mahal and in order for it not to go under it would have to do what no other casino had ever done: make a million dollars a day. His father, Fred Trump, would buy three million dollars' worth of chips to try and help his son but it would be to no avail.

Trump would end up having to file for bankruptcy on the great building. The real estate mogul would experience his first defeat and failure.

He would eventually accrue debt for a billion dollars; but Trump would end up filing for corporate bankruptcy six times. He would do whatever he had to in order to keep from going under. He would file for the first time in 1991 and then again in 1992; and then file three more times. He would struggle to stay on his feet. And even when he struggled it could not be detected with the "naked eye." Trump believed that it didn't matter if you got knocked down in life. What mattered was that no matter how hard you are hit, you better know how to get back up and fight again. He got back up but in 2004 and 2009 Trump filed for bankruptcy; but corporate bankruptcy only, never for personal bankruptcy.

Trump was forced to file his first corporate bankruptcy a year after the Trump organization financed—with risky, high interest "junk bonds"—the construction of Trump Taj Mahal Casino in Atlantic City, New Jersey. The casino was reportedly almost $3 billion dollars in debt. At that point, after bragging it was doing well, Trump would be forced to file for Chapter 11 bankruptcy protection. That is, his company's managers would continue to run the company while they are negotiating with their creditors, trying to convince them how the debt would be repaid. His company then makes a proposal on reorganizing a better plan which will need to be approved by the creditors and the bankruptcy court.

When Trump had to file again in 1992, it was for the Trump Castle, the Trump Plaza and Casino in Atlantic City, and the Plaza Hotel in New York. It was looking as if everything that glittered was not gold. It was all sunshine on the way up but once in business it all came crashing down; and Trump fell hard. And, in 2004, Trump had to file bankruptcy again. This time it was for the Trump Hotel and Casino Resorts which were almost $2 billion dollars in debt. However, in 2009 he filed again, giving protection to Trump Entertainment resorts. But again, Trump figured a way out and was soon back on top.

"Failure is not an option."

Not His First Choice

It didn't take long for the young Trump to build a real estate empire in Manhattan. He did it in style and with speed, making it look easy. His father was young Donald's mentor. "He was a special guy, strong, smart and my best friend," Donald would say. "He loved detail and order; he built on time; we had the same qualities." His father built houses but

Donald built skyscrapers. When asked if he tried to outdo his father, he responded, "No, I don't think so. That was never my intention." Trump decided on his first project when he spotted his first building. He saw a vision of what he could do with the building, how he could improve the building, but also how he could improve all of Manhattan City. "He was very proud of me. He lived until almost 94 years old so he saw a lot of it."

Although Trump became an overnight success and real estate mogul, his first choice was not real estate. He attended business school with the intention to make movies. "At first, I wanted to make movies. I've always liked the glamor of movies. If you can make it in one business, you can be successful in other businesses." But he would end up following in his father's footsteps into the real estate game. "Real estate was easy for me; get the best location, make the best deal, get it done on time and it's a success," The Donald would say. He was so good at business that he was awarded The Entrepreneur award from school. He attributes his success to having good parents and a good family. He actually said they were a great family. "I realized in my first 12 years the value of great parents and good family." He didn't grow up poor. He lived in a huge house; his father was a millionaire. "My mother would threaten to whoop me with a wooden spoon when I was bad, but she never did it."

At 13, his father sent him off to military school—the New York Military Academy. "As a kid I was rebellious, smart, was very rambunctious and talked out of turn." His father felt he needed structure which he did because the Academy had a good impact on him. "I became a Captain and graduated at the highest level." In April 1998, on the "Oprah" show, Oprah asked Donald if he would ever run for President. "If it got so bad I would." Trump pretty much said no because he liked the life he had—the power, the freedom, the celebrity status and the riches. But then, on another occasion, he said he might run for President one day. Nobody took him seriously.

"I know when people tell him it can't be done, that guarantees that he will get it done. I know that when someone tells him that something is impossible, that's what triggers him into action."
— Donald Trump, Jr.

Chapter Seven

In Fear

The National Basketball League stopped using Trump Hotels. Trump businesses began to lose money. The Mexican people are living in fear that the local and federal police will kick down their doors to question, to handcuff, to arrest and take their family members to jail to face deportation. The world is in a panic. For the first time in decades, since the days of Hitler and the Jim Crow Laws, people are uncertain about their future. Muslims are living in fear of being attacked or being labeled a terrorist. Immigrants who own homes and businesses have no clue what will happen to their establishments if they are arrested and deported. But their main concerns are for their children born in the United States. Will they be considered U.S. citizens or will they be considered illegal citizens?

Will their families be split-up and if so, will they ever see them again? These are the questions racing through the minds of the uncertain. Immigrants are frantically running around trying to get married to an American citizen so they can become legal and not wake up, living in fear.

And Trump is unapologetic about it all. White people are driving by in their cars yelling, "nigger" and "wetback" again; constantly telling Mexicans to go home. Donald Trump is the new dictator in the United States and he is building a vicious army of people around him who have racist backgrounds. He appointed Jeff Sessions as attorney general who is known for his racist comments. And, he appointed Michael Flynn as his National Security Advisor who screamed "lock her [Hillary] up" and "all cultures should not be treated the same." He also appointed Michael Pompeo as head of the CIA. This was terrible news for the Republicans, America and the world. Pompeo believes that America's power is viewed as diminished and that the military must be beefed up.

Trump has turned the political world upside down. His supporters are ready to shed blood to defend him. Two thugs in Boston literally beat down a homeless Hispanic man with an iron bar and quoted some of Donald Trump's rhetoric to the police as their justification for the crime. Another aged Trump supporter in North Carolina assaulted a protestor. Afterwards, in Las Vegas, Trump himself screamed, "I'd like to punch him in the face!" When Trump was interrupted by a Black Lives Matter protestor, it almost caused a race riot. He has also turned against the media and surprisingly none of the journalists have been beaten down by the way Trump has insulted them. "Some of the most dishonest people in the world," he has called them.

He appears threatening and vile to the media to the people he is surrounding himself with. It is disturbing and he is obviously not trying to bring the country together. Some commentators say he is a fascist, an idea he encouraged by inviting his followers to pledge their allegiance to him with a fascist-style salute at a rally in Florida. These are the same attributes that Adolph Hitler had. A significant minority of his supporters (17%) consider ethnic diversity bad for America. And Trump's immigration idea to build the wall appeals to them. "Build the wall! Build the wall! Build the wall! Build the wall!" his supporters shouted. It's no wonder 86% of African-Americans and 80% of Hispanics have a very negative view of him. If he could just go door-to-door and murder all immigrants as Hitler and his German army did, he possibly would. With Donald Trump as the new dictator, America is now living in fear. He gives the impression that he would have the police going door-to-door to seek out illegal immigrants and have them locked up and deported.

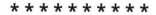

People are confused and uncertain about the new change. They are indecisive about their future; not knowing what to tell children who have a white mother and black father. In school a Spanish teacher addressed her class. "Okay children, sit down. Class is about to start." But a 4th grade white child looked at her in disgust and said, "I don't have to listen to you no more. You ain't even from here. You got to go back home!" It crushed her heart. The parents and the President are now turning their kids against other races. It's a known fact that immigrants work hard after they make it over the wall to get here.

To build his Trump Tower he would end up facing lawsuits and accusations of employing undocumented workers. The very same people

Trump called rapists are the same people he used to build his buildings. Therefore, they were a huge contribution to his success. The same people he is trying to deport, to build a wall to keep them out are the same people he used to his advantage. He underpaid them, used them and now he has decided to throw them away and send them back to where they came from because they are no longer needed. It is Trump's belief that Mexico sends their people to the United States that they don't want: the rapists, the criminals or those with criminal intentions. Minority groups are coming together to form a coalition to fight against Trump.

The police are on the news trying to bring calm to the people. "We will not be coming to your homes looking for people, checking papers and trying to deport them. It is not a problem for the local police. If it does happen it will be the feds and not the local police," the police said. But it did not ease the people's fears. Mexico has said they are prepared to accept all their people who will be sent back. The world is in chaos under the new leadership of Donald Trump, who, just like Hitler, feels that his race is the supreme race. Black America is raining tears and the fear of the unknown is slowly torturing them. Their hearts race anytime a police vehicle is behind them or a policeman looks their way. When they hear sirens they think it is for them.

Immigrants and Muslims are now afraid to call 9-1-1 and report a crime out of fear of being discovered and deported. They no longer feel free in this country but hunted as if every immigrant has a warrant out for their arrest. It's to the point where they are afraid to make direct eye contact with the police. Kids at school are beating up kids they've known all their lives just because they like Trump or are wearing a Trump t-shirt, while other kids are protesting and refusing to go to class. People are on TV crying, including Miley Cyrus. They are afraid and scared; in fear for tomorrow.

But the mayors' of New York City, Philadelphia, Los Angeles and Chicago, among other cities, tried to console the bleeding hearts and pain of the immigrants by announcing to the world that their cities would always be a sanctuary city where people could be safe, including all immigrants. "We will not cooperate with Donald Trump's laws!" the mayors told their citizens. But the Trump administration responded by saying, "Chicago has the highest murder rate in America right now. How are people safe?" It was true that in 2016 Chicago had a high rate of shootings and murders among African-Americans, which included a retaliation killing of a nine-year-old boy. Although the good people of America are trying to show compassion, it did very little to ease their fears. The world seems to be going crazy and it is true about Chicago being the murder capital of America. One weekend, 17 people were killed and more than 40 people injured. All victims were from African-American neighborhoods. Chicago is the nation's 3rd largest city, and that weekend marked the deadliest weekend in what had been the city's most violent year in a decade. But the city was still trying to convince everyone that their immigrants would be safe. But because of Trump there are several cities whose murder rate has skyrocketed. TRUMP DIDN'T MAKE AMERICA GREAT AGAIN — HE MADE AMERICA HATE AGAIN! AND HE WASN'T EVEN THE PRESIDENT YET.

"He was just black in the wrong place."
— Valerie Castile

"In times of turmoil, in times of uncertainty,
in times of strife, hate crimes increase."
— LA Police Chief, Charlie Beck

Chapter Eight

Reality TV Star

In 2004, Trump filed for corporate bankruptcy but that $2 million dollar debt was only a snag in Trump's business. In 2004, Trump quickly devised a new way to get more money. It was the first year of the reality television series "The Apprentice" where Trump was the host. Trump would offer prospective up and coming executives a chance to win a prominent position in the Trump organization. From 2008 until 2009 celebrities started to compete as apprentices but the show decided to go back to the original format which had made it a success. But again, in 2010, the show would return to the celebrity format and the show's name changed to "Celebrity Apprentice." Trump left the show in 2015 after announcing his run for president.

After Trump called Mexicans rapists and criminals, NBC which aired the show severed ties with Trump. Also, because of those remarks, Trump had to make a business decision to sell the Miss Universe organization after the Spanish TV network, Univision, refused to air the Miss USA Pageants. But again, Trump boasted he would make even more money because his contract was violated. So he confessed no worries.

One-n-the Same

Trump, just like Hitler himself on occasion, is charming, unpredictable, a leader of men and thirsty for power. Trump, as was Hitler, is in charge of the military and wanted to have the most powerful army in the world. Trump does differ from Hitler in some ways but that's not unusual. He differs from many men. He is the first billionaire President the world has ever had; the first President to have his name displayed on skyscrapers all throughout New York and other major cities; the first President to have casinos. He is a master at real estate and business. When he ran for President he broke down the blue wall as he masterminded an unconventional campaign that's never been presented before. He was an unprecedented candidate yet he still became President of the United States.

"BELIEVE ME, GENERAL I AM THE GREATEST BUILDER OF FORTIFICATIONS OF ALL TIME. I BUILT THE WEST WALL," Hitler told Colonel-General Guderian in January 1944. Just like Hitler, Trump professed to build a wall. Steve Bannon, a "Breitbart" executive who was in charge of cleaning up Trump's racist image, stated, "I don't want my kids to go to school with Jews!" Just as Hitler detested Jews, Trump would surround himself with people who had the same racist mentality. Hitler's vision was to "MAKE GERMANY GREAT AGAIN." It is the same slogan Trump would use when he ran for President in 2016. Trump would say, "LET'S MAKE AMERICA GREAT AGAIN," with whites in their 60's, 70's, and 80's, cheering him on. They are the same people who once lived during the time of the Jim Crow Laws, during segregation and before integration. Some of them had lived during the times of Hitler as well. However, even though America had changed, they had not.

Hitler would preach propaganda, spreading his ideas to further his cause of how the Germans were the supreme race and how he didn't like Jews who, at the time, were predominantly running Germany. The Jews had the money, the businesses, the power and high positions. Although the Germans were in power as senators, governors and in Congress, they would cater to the Jews. But Hitler didn't like it and he was tired of it. He wasn't a man who would bite his tongue when speaking. Like Trump, he said whatever came into his mind. He was unpredictable and kept everyone off-balance. He was very outspoken about how he felt and what he believed in. He went to jail for preaching propaganda but that didn't stop him. He would tell anybody who would listen, "Germany needs to be in power!" He would express to his followers it was Hitler who created the Nazi sign. He was willing to die for what he believed in. Hitler would eventually form groups who were in poverty. Trump would do the same thing by targeting the poor whites that the world forgot about. They would use the same tactics to accomplish their ultimate goals.

When Hitler got out of jail he kept preaching his ideas and just like with Trump, more and more people started to listen. His group of followers began to increase. One thing Hitler decided while in jail; he would get his followers and storm the building that held the men who were in power. His entire goal was to take over the military. But to do that he had to seize the men who were in control. He had given it a lot of thought. So once he amassed his followers, he sprang into action. Hitler and his group of men stormed the building. "Get down! Get the fuck on the ground." They ran inside, screaming and attacking. But they were no match for the military which would eventually overpower his army. They waged a small war of Germans against Germans, but Hitler would lose and go to jail again.

In jail he would suffer in pain and confusion, wondering why the Germans did not see what he clearly saw. But Hitler, like Trump, would stop at nothing to see his vision become a reality. "Build the wall! Build the wall!" was echoed during the days of Hitler. On January 30, 1933 it was bragged that the new Nationalist Socialist Empire was founded and it would last a thousand years. But it didn't work out that way. It actually lasted only 12 years and four months. Behind it, Hitler's boasted, "1,000 Year Reich" left nothing solid except the consequences people suffered for the worst geographical and political war in history, and of course that lasting monument built in concrete and steel. The same monument Donald J. Trump brags about: The Great Wall. It was built by Adolf Hitler himself. It was also called The Siegfried Line by his western allies. It's been fifty years after the evil genius completed The Wall and now in 2016 another man stands in front of the world screaming, "I will build a wall!"

The Wall was ordered for construction. It traveled across the German countryside from the border through the flat plains of Holland. It would pass France, Luxembourg and Belgium for hundreds of miles. It was so thick and tall that nobody could get over it. It stayed up for almost 40 years. It was still strong after several attempts to destroy it in subsequent wars which included allied nations. The military roads filled with potholes, wrecked bunkers, dragon's teeth, and the steel spars beneath the hedgerows-stark weathered monuments to a terrible past, will still be there when the last survivor of the impossible dream—the 1,000 Year Reich—is long, long dead, according to Whiting (the Nazi's last stand).

But Trump wants to repeat history and keep out the people who don't have blue eyes and blond hair. Just like Hitler, he vowed to make Germany great again and he wanted the blue-eyed man with blond hair to be supreme. The confusing part about Hitler was that he wasn't even a real German. It wasn't until 1928 that Adolf Hitler started to accept

German nationality. He was forty years old. But he believed two things: Germans were the supreme race and Germany needed to be great again. And to do that, he would have to go to war.

When Hitler was again released from jail he had a plan—he would get out, continue spreading the word and build a stronger army. He would also get inside the heads of men who served in the military but were still living poorly. Hitler would tell them they deserved more. They started taking heed to his words and Hitler's army began to grow. When he believed it was strong enough, he attacked the men in power again. He stormed into the building with his army and this time it was different. They captured everyone: senators, governors and those in Congress. This time men from the military chose to stand by his side. Hitler would arrest those in power as he prepared to become Germany's new dictator, just as Donald Trump became America's new President.

*"Know who you are dealing with.
Do not offend the wrong person."*
— *Robert Greene*

Chapter Nine

Mexico

After several months of yelling, "I'm going to build a wall," Trump announced he was going to Mexico. He shocked the world again. They wondered to themselves why would he go to Mexico after denigrating their people and country? He had called them criminals, rapists and murderers. He said he would build a wall and make them pay for it. He said that Mexico sent all their bad people to America and he just abused them for almost a year. But in August of 2016, he would go to Mexico to meet with Mexican President Enrique Peña Nieto. Nobody could figure out what he was thinking but the meeting did not go as he probably planned it.

During the entire meeting Trump was walking on ice as he contradicted all the insults he'd made about Mexico and backpedaling on some of his explosive remarks. "We will not pay for a wall!" President Nieto adamantly told Trump who did not dispute it. Nieto was firm and direct—Mexico would not pay for any wall. Hillary said during the debate as well as to the media, "Trump choked when he was face-to-face with President Nieto who stated he would not pay for any wall. He said nothing." When Trump was questioned about it he said, "We discussed the wall. We didn't discuss payment." After bashing Mexico and its people he told the world, "It was a great honor to be invited to the Presidential residence by Nieto," who he all of a sudden now calls a friend. The people began to wonder if he couldn't stand up to Mexico, how can he stand up to Russia or China?

But soon after leaving Mexico he made his way to Arizona and again reiterated his famous immigration speech, adding additional words. "Mexico will pay for the wall!" he shouted confidently. "They just don't know it yet, but they're going to pay for it. And after giving it serious thought, Nieto said, "I regret my very rushed decision to meet this summer with Republican nominee Donald Trump." The meeting was widely attacked in Mexico and the critics accused Nieto of lending "gravitas" to a man who blatantly called

Mexicans criminals and rapists. Nieto's finance minister and close ally, Luis Videgaray was quickly forced to resign his position. Many media reports emerged that it was Videgaray who urged the meeting after several ministers had objected overall. The meeting made it appear as if Trump could call Mexican's negative names and then had the balls to go and meet with them.

"Could we have done things better? Maybe, yes. Ultimately, Mexico will have to build a relationship with whoever is elected President."

— *Enrique Peña Nieto*

Groped By Trump

"When you're rich and powerful, I just do it. They don't care," Trump brags while being secretly taped. Women started surfacing from everywhere saying that Trump groped them or made sexual advances towards them. It started with two women who said Trump had absolutely lied on national TV during the second Presidential debate when he said, "I never groped a woman," although there was a recording from 2005 of him contradicting that statement according to a published report by the New York Times. A Manhattan resident by the name of Jessica Leeds, age 74 at the time, told the New York Times, "I wanted to punch the screen when he said that! He grabbed my breast and tried to put his hand up my skirt during a flight to New York." She said it happened more than 30 years ago. "He was like an octopus. Of course, I was only 38 back then."

Another victim who accused Trump in 2005 was only 22, young and pretty, exactly how he liked them. She told the New York Times, "Trump forcibly kissed me when I introduced myself to him outside a Trump Tower elevator." Her name is Rachel Crooks. Of course Trump denied the accusations and called the women liars. He also threatened to sue the women for defamation of his character. Trump's communications advisor, Jason Miller, called the article "fiction." He said, "To reach back decades in an attempt to smear Mr. Trump trivializes sexual assault and sets a new low for where the media is willing to go in its efforts to determine this election." Those statements made several of Trump's surrogates cancel appearances on news talk shows.

But Mayor Rudy Giuliani would not abandon Trump and relished the role as Trump's defender.

"Men, at times, talk like that," he told CNN, referring to Trump. The next day when he spoke at a rally Giuliani jokingly implied, in Trump's defense, that his comments were merely "locker room talk." He brushed it off as if it was nothing even though it was a habit of Trump's to overstep boundaries of sexual propriety, including his past boasts about grabbing women's genitals and kissing women against their will.

During the first GOP primary debate Fox News host, Megyn Kelly, asked the great Trump about his treatment of women, repeating comments where he called them "pigs" and "slobs." Trump responded, "Only if it's Rosie O'Donnell." Afterwards he would go on to Tweet his supporters, calling Kelly a "bimbo" and suggested she had "blood coming out of her eyes; blood coming out of her whatever." He also spoke badly about executive Carly Fiorina by saying, "Look at that face. Would anyone vote for that?" And he said Hillary "got schlonged"—Yiddish slang for the male sex organ— by Obama in the 2008 Democratic primary. "This is disgraceful. It is intolerable and it doesn't matter what party you belong to whether Democrat, Republic or Independent. No woman deserves to be treated this way," said Michelle Obama. "It's unforgivable for 'family values' Christian leaders to support Trump in light of these assault allegations. Women are viewing this as a betrayal." French said, "If you can endorse Donald Trump, it's an albatross around your neck for the rest of your political career."

AMP

American   Money   Publishing

WE PUBLISH THE REALIST BOOKS

Chapter Ten

Recent Trump Accusers

Trump has an aura so strong that one of his women supporters said, "I resent Trump's accusers for conveniently waiting until the last month of the Presidential election to come forward with their accusations. And I can't stand the way Clinton handled the sexual allegations against her husband when she was first lady. It's not that Trump's actions don't bother me," she said, "it's that her actions bother me, too." It's almost like there's a higher accountability in being a woman. The female population is too large to boil down to a political bloc. And it appears that a lot of them resent any implication that their vote should be determined by their gender. Some of the women even believed the media distorted Trump's words. They were more focused on the Clinton email situation which they believed was more of a betrayal and more appalling.

Through media interviews the world was witnessing over and over again a woman being castigated. What they saw was a double standard shown by the way people reacted to the accusations to Trump versus how they reacted to Bill Clinton. The outrage was extremely different when Paula Jones accused Clinton of exposing himself and when Kathleen Willey accused Clinton of groping her there was no huge outrage or, when Juanita Broaddrick accused Bill of rape. "None of the same female leaders who rallied around Anita Hill when Supreme Court nominee Clarence Thomas was accused of sexual harassment voiced their outcry about Bill Clinton's accusations. A woman spoke out. "Why are we attacking the Republican candidate for something that isn't nearly as inflammatory as something that's been done in the past?" Toria Morgan, a Trump supporter said, "He's not been proven to be guilty of anything." Jan Horne stated, "We can look at him under a microscope and look at her under a telescope. That's the only way they can compare them."

But Hillary feels that not only has he disrespected veterans, called Mexicans rapists, says

Muslims are all terrorists, been disgusting and dishonest, she feels women have always been his biggest targets. "He loves beauty contests, supporting them and hanging around them. He even called Alicia Machado, a former Miss Universe, Miss Piggy." But none of that criticism fazed Trump. He responded with, "That bitch and Hillary sucks. But not like Monica (referring to Monica Lewinsky who reportedly had oral sex with Bill Clinton)." It would appear with that kind of talk from a Presidential nominee, he would lose support. But with Trump it was just the opposite.

His supporters took particular glee in his outrageous attacks. They were viewed as a new refreshing breath of air in a world choking on political correctness. It was like he could do no wrong no matter what rolled off his tongue of venom. His supporters loved it and became stronger believers in the billionaire real estate mogul. "Politics is capturing what's happening in every other place in society." Myers went on to say, "This election is defined around the fundamental conflict not between men and women but between patriarchy and feminism." Trump stated Hillary was playing the woman card and other women were coming to her defense. "We want men to be men and women to be women," said Bobbie Frantz, a Trump supporter who says she's a feminist. "We want to be strong women but we don't want to take over the role of men." But the former Secretary of State, Madeleine Albright, blustered back, "Just remember, there's a special place in hell for women who don't help each other."

Megyn Kelly stated, "He came after me like a dog with a bone for nine months." He called women disgusting animals and Ivana Trump said, "He raped me," but then recanted and took it back. Megyn wrote about his treatment of her in her book which the world said she should have released before the election. But Tamara Neo didn't want to hear it. "His mistreatment of women was outweighed by all his other good issues." Tamara Neo said she voted for him regardless of what those women said. With all the different accusations and silent, untold stories it's obvious Trump is not just a sexist pig, he is a sexual predator who takes advantage of women, using his money and power. And he has waged war on the women who have accused him.

Condemned in Public

When Trump used Bill Clinton as a comparison and the media exposed it, Hillary defended her husband and played a major role in helping him escape his consequences. Then when it came to her email scandal, she continued to elude justice by skating past topics related to her emails. Republican and Trump believed that her handling of classified material was "extremely careless," according to FBI Director James Comey. This conclusion would normally be enough to get anybody else who wasn't a Clinton, fired or arrested. Trump vowed that when he became President he would appoint a special prosecutor to charge her, arrest her and lock her up. "Lock her up! Lock her up! Lock her up!" his supporters would chant. Trump said, "She is crooked Hillary and she deserves to go to jail."

Trump tried to water down his tape recording from the "Access Hollywood" bus and the accusations from other women of groping and sexual assault. He hadn't realized that sexual mistreatment had changed in the eyes of the public. Look at Bill Cosby and Roger Ailes. It has become front page news and people can go to jail for it. It is no longer discussed outside the context of violent attacks by strangers. Universities, sports leagues and major institutions to media empires are now forced to battle with their own policies of tolerating sexual misconduct. "No means no" rather than "no means yes" is becoming the new standard on most college campuses. What Americans once tolerated in the shadows is now an issue that any man, especially powerful ones, will be condemned in public. But Trump is Trump and no matter what he did and no matter how hard the media tried to tarnish Trump's character, he only became more and more popular. Although he did lose the popular vote to Hillary, he was very popular among his supporters. The media did all they could to condemn Trump but it seemed as if he was beyond condemnation. His tarnished character would actually catapult him to victory.

American   Money   Publishing

WE PUBLISH THE REALIST BOOKS

Chapter Eleven

The Divide

Trump has divided the country. People are divided from around the world, from city to city and from state to state. You can see division in the workplace, among friends, within households and even between husbands and wives. These difficult discussions are being talked about everywhere among everybody. It's a decision of who chooses who. "I can't join my husband in voting for Trump. I just can't," a woman said. "I'm a Republican but I can't vote my normal vote for the GOP. I can't because he's Donald Trump." The division has turned ugly, so ugly that friends, co-workers, husbands and wives and even church members have become enemies. An Atlanta Christian nonprofit worker, Ruth Maihorta, believed that her church congregation had always been like her family. But the once friendly faces had become not so friendly, even to the point of becoming hostile and disrespectful.

Maihorta was the only member who refused to vote for Trump and she was ostracized, ridiculed and screamed at by people she thought once loved her. She was interrogated by church ushers; on Facebook she was harassed by her own fellow congregants and denigrated because she chose not to vote for Trump. It was all confusing because she once thought of these people as friends, spiritual mentors, brothers and sisters. But now they were saying, "We're ashamed of you. You need to get right with God." They felt that my insulting Trump would only help Hillary who they believed was a baby killer. "Don't you know that by not siding with Trump you have sided with Satan!" one of her congregants said. Her Facebook page was bombarded with hateful comments, distasteful rhetoric and unsavory remarks. But some of her liberal friends would try to comfort her, backing her right of choice. "It's made for strange bedfellows," she expressed. "It's made me more understanding of people who are not like me politically. And I've started to extend more grace to those views because I wish the pro-Trump people would extend more grace to me." But they wouldn't. One of the comments was so disturbing that she shared it with a friend. Surprisingly, she found herself repeating a quote from then First Lady Michelle Obama. "When they go low, we go high."

This type of division was happening everywhere throughout the country. While Trump was screaming, "Let's make America great again," he was actually ripping it apart. Teenagers were bullying and beating up their friends whom they had known all their lives for wearing a Trump t-shirt. Kids were turning against teachers; people were marching in cities across the nation protesting against Trump; husbands and wives were fighting each other and filing for divorce. Whites believed in Trump while blacks despised him. Democrats and Republicans were fighting like cats and dogs to the point it had Hillary yelling to the world, "Trump is not fit to be President." It was so bad that children sometimes became estranged from their parents. Mothers and daughters had differing opinions and one decided to move out or not visit the other. Fathers and sons had the same problem. At Thanksgiving mothers and fathers and some relatives decided not to show up to avoid conflict.

Then there was the little grandson who was mixed with black and his black father no longer felt accepted by his white wife's family. Trump had brought out the family's old racist feelings and no one could hide them. The nation was no longer progressing. It was regressing under Trump. It was not moving forward but moving backward. "God help us," people were saying. "Why is this happening?" confused young people would ask not having grown up hating any race. There were a lot of sad and crying faces from not knowing what their relationships with their family would become. America is now wracked by division. The country is in chaos with race-baiting, hatred and dissatisfied voters. The world doesn't trust Hillary Clinton and they believe Donald Trump is a racist, billionaire white man who wants to "take back the country."

The Ku Klux Klan's official newspaper touted front page support for Trump. White folks are bombing black churches while white police officers are killing black unarmed men. Some of these officers have pledged to be Trump supporters. On the other hand, Hillary Clinton is being accused of having alleged connections to corruption in Washington insider practices. Neither presidential contender has convinced the world that they have a vision for a stronger united future. "Reuniting is up to the people of the United States," said former U.S. Congresswoman and Presidential Candidate Cynthia McKinney. But uniting seems a faraway goal for Americans with such drastic views and different allegiances. Cattiness between and against the candidates fed the violence at Trump's rallies; including volatile rhetoric and the verbal threats of more violence in post-election American society.

The Nation of Islam's, Minister Louis Farrakhan, stated, "If Satan cast out Satan, his house is divided against himself. How then will his kingdom stand?" If the divided house cannot stand, it is doomed to fall. America is now dissatisfied, divided and doomed from the way things are looking. "I want to say to my friends who are with Mrs. Clinton, and some other of my friends who are with Bernie Sanders and some other of my friends who are with Mr. Trump. We are not going to lose any friendships over white people that want to continue to rule us," Farrakhan said in a message delivered from Mosque Maryam in Chicago. "The bigger picture is the black masses of America and the American people whose lives are at stake," he continued. "Now the scripture is being fulfilled wherein it prophesies that in these days, meaning the end of the wicked world of Satan: rulers are against rulers, kings against kings, nations against nations. In the days of the prophets there were no heads of government who were given the name 'President'; rulers were referred to as rulers and kings as kings of the people. The prediction of the prophets who wrote our future before we lived is now coming to pass."

It was so quiet in the room you could hear a pin drop as Farrakhan expressed what he believed was happening in the United States. "America is now being torn to pieces politically as Pharaoh's political party was in the days when Jehovah went after the freedom of the children of Israel. Egypt was plagued with drought, great hailstorms, rain and fire, according to the Psalm of David. 'Running side-by-side, fire and water.' These plagues are now visiting America from Almighty God Allah." Because of all the violence, the FBI has opened a civil rights investigation on the vandalism of a black church in Mississippi where the words, "Vote Trump," was spray-painted on an outside wall. The fire was deliberately set and blackened the sanctuary's pews, pulpit and walls. Only the shell of the church was left standing. It was estimated that 80% of the church was burned according to Chief Fireman Ruben Brown. Authorities also offered an $11 thousand dollar reward for information leading to the arrest and conviction of the culprit.

A former Congress woman who is black, is considering making changes after witnessing Trump ruin the Republican party structure and support base. "I don't know how long that's going to last but it's not an accident for us to watch. As a result of Trump's wrecking ball, all of the slime has slithered over to the Democratic Party. And so now you've got the very people who Democrats fought are now supporting the Democratic nominee." McKinney said. It's very possible that the country might never heal from this division that Trump created. He didn't want to make America great again, it appears he wanted "to make America hate again" which included Peter Thiel and the tech giants on the board of Facebook.

"After eight years as your President, I still believe there is so much more that unites us than divides us."
— President Barack Obama

Chapter Twelve

Unpredictability

Trump's signature dress style is a dark suit with a red or blue tie. He gives off an aura of someone with power and who is very important. Trump didn't become a billionaire twice because he was stupid. He became a billionaire twice because he knows the secret to outsmarting people. Ninety-nine percent of people will never become a billionaire in their lifetime, but Donald J. Trump has done it twice. The man is a genius and has mastered the ability to not be figured out. Humans are creations of habit. It confuses them when they don't see familiarity in a person. The world is used to predictability; it gives them a sense of control. But when someone emerges who does things that are abnormal and unpredictable, it throws the average person for a loop. They become confused and unsure as to how to deal with the person. That person is Trump.

Trump is deliberately unpredictable. There is nothing consistent about his behavior except making money. He keeps everyone off-balance; no one ever knows what he might do or what type of lewd language might come out of his mouth. He skipped a debate on purpose and told everyone he was going to do it. That was unheard of. Trump was making his own rules. He called Mitt Romney a choke artist and revealed Lindsay Graham's phone number. Who does that? He refused to accept advice or read the teleprompter. He's had the entire world wearing themselves out trying to understand his behavior. Trump's enemies have become confused. He's talked about China and how they were robbing America, raping America and how they had no respect for America. He said he would build a wall and make Mexico pay for it. "When I'm done talking they will beg to pay for it," he told everyone.

Trump is an extremist with strategies that would intimidate and terrorize the average person. He doesn't just look for the best move; he looks for the move that will disturb his opponent while destroying him or her. Trump played the polls and the world like a game of chess because Trump understands that chess contains the concentrated essence of life: First, to win, you must be patient and farseeing; secondly, because the game is built on patterns, entire sequences of moves have been played before and will be played again, with slight alterations in any one match. Your opponent analyzes the patterns you are playing and then try to foresee your moves; allowing your opponent nothing predictable to base their strategy upon gives you a big advantage. In chess, as in life, when people can't figure out what you are doing they are kept in a state of terror—waiting, uncertain, confused.

Nothing is more terrifying than the sudden and the unpredictable. This is the reason why tornadoes and earthquakes frighten us so much. We do not know when they will strike. After a disaster has occurred we wait in terror for the next one. To a lesser degree, this is the effect that unpredictable human behavior has on us. This is the effect Donald J. Trump has on us.

"Law #17 – Keep others in suspended terror. Cultivate an air of unpredictability."

— *Robert Greene*

Allan Lichtman, although Trump was unpredictable, predicted that Trump would win the presidency. His predictions had also been right in a few previous elections. He has also predicted that Trump will be impeached. The main stream media wanted Trump to fail when it was reported that Hillary was winning in the polls. But they were wrong at every turn of the election. They said he would never win but they were all wrong. How could Allan Lichtman make such a prediction after Trump had offended every type of group possible? No President had disrespected so many groups and blatantly denigrated so many people. Trump insulted and groped women; he insulted immigrants, Muslims, Whoopi Goldberg, Germany, Ronda Rousey and the Pope. He impersonated Chinese leaders in a disrespectful way. "We want a deal!" he would mimic. He performed a distasteful imitation of a handicapped person and Tweeted a claim that 81% of whites were killed by blacks which was an outright lie. The number of whites killed by blacks is below 15%. But after all that, including disrespecting a war hero, Trump still won. That's unpredictable and unbelievable.

"Humans are creatures of habit with an insatiable need to see familiarity in other people's actions."

— *Robert Greene*

Birth of theTrumps

His success and love for publicity make him one of the most talked about figures in business. As the President, Chairman and Chief Executive Officer of the Trump Organization, Trump bought and sold many major buildings, mostly skyscrapers and mostly in New York City. Then he decided to venture into television, first with small parts where he played himself then while hosting his popular reality series "The Apprentice," where he gained more fame. Donald's father, Fred Trump, was his inspiration. Fred Trump was born in the United States to German immigrants. Young Donald's paternal grandfather, Friedrich Trump was born in 1869 in Germany. He made a decision to migrate to the United States in the 1880's. He was determined to make a better life for the Trump's and himself. He started his chain of hotels and restaurants in the western United States and Canada to serve the miners heading to the Klondike Gold Rush in the Yukon region of Canada.

His grandfather became a U.S. citizen (changed his name to Frederick), returned to Germany and met his future wife (and Donald's grandmother), Elizabeth Christ. They would get married in 1902 and move to the United States. They had three children which included Donald's father, Frederick Christ Trump.

Donald's mother, Mary Anne MacLeod, was born in Scotland. In 1930, she would migrate to New York City where she met Donald's father. They met at a dance, immediately fell in love and soon became man and wife.

Fred Trump was the backbone of his family which caused Donald to view him as a domineering man with a god-like persona. Trump's father built a fortune in the 1920's as a real estate developer of single-family homes in the City of New York and Queens. His first son, Frederick Trump, was expected to be the successor of the Trump businesses. But Frederick couldn't cut it. He wasn't blessed with the gift to be a successful businessman. He did try but his failures led him to drink excessively and he soon became an alcoholic. He soon left the real estate business after not measuring up to his father's expectations. He made an attempt to try his hand at becoming a commercial pilot, but his addiction would get the best of him. In 1981, at the age of only 42, Donald and the Trump family would have to bury Freddy Trump. His father would lose a son and Donald would lose his older brother. Because of the death of Freddy, Donald vowed to never drink alcohol and until this day he hasn't. Trump respected his father and he liked that he was a Trump. He liked how people treated and respected his father and he vowed to make sure the Trump name would always keep that respect.

"So much depends on reputation.
Guard it with your life."
— *Robert Greene*

"In that family you're either a winner or loser."
— *Patterson*

Chapter Thirteen

Fantasy

Trump was able to tap into the masses of people's fantasies. He would tell them what he knew they wanted to hear. He knew white and black people were tired of all the foreign people coming into the United States and taking opportunities away from them. He knew they were tired of immigrants crossing the borders and taking all the jobs by working for lower wages. They were tired of the Mexicans robbing, stealing, raping and gangbanging once they crossed into the United States. Although Trump knew he could not and would not build a wall like he promised, he knew that's what the people wanted to hear. He could not tell the truth because the truth was ugly and not what the people wanted to hear. He said he would cut taxes by lowering them lower than they'd ever been and stop Muslims from entering the U.S. from foreign countries. He said he would deport all illegal immigrants back to their own countries.

He knew Hillary would speak the truth even though he called her a liar. He knew that she would only say things that she would do if she felt and believed they were doable. But not Trump. He said whatever he wanted to with little regard to who it would hurt. He didn't want the traditional voters who always voted. He wanted the voters who felt they were always overlooked and nobody cared about them. Trump also tapped into the haters of other races; the ones with a Ku Klux Klan mentality; the white supremacist groups and the poor who wanted to make more money. He knew the truth would only make them angry and disenchanted. He pointed out the flaws of America; the dark and distasteful state the country was now in. Trump made them believe he felt the same way they did and if they elected him he would MAKE AMERICA GREAT AGAIN.

Whenever he talked about men and women without jobs or being underpaid, he focused on certain types of jobs: the less skilled but well-paying union jobs that have been eradicated by the advance of technology and globalization. Those were the jobs that at one time were considered the "elite" jobs Americans could live comfortably from. They were once Americans who could live off a single income. But over the past two decades employment in manufacturing and utilities declined. And without college degrees those Americans were left behind. The economic shift declined by 30% and hastily became a man size crisis. "This is an election about the loss of the jobs that allowed them to feel like successful men," explained Andrew Cherlin, a Johns Hopkins University sociologist and author of *Labor's Love Lost*. With the loss of those jobs people not only lost their jobs, they lost their self-esteem; and their hope of living the American dream slowly slipped away.

But when Trump emerged they had hope again. Finally, someone understood their pain. The white men without college degrees had felt defeated and found themselves on the losing end of change in America. However, former President George W. Bush said, "Anger shouldn't drive policy. People should vote in what's best." Trump told his supporters, "Extreme vetting for refugees is an ISIS threat. Radical Islamic terror is right around the corner. We must stop them from coming in!" This was exactly what his supporters wanted to hear.

Trump described his campaign as a movement and people from all over were getting on board.

Bob Holmes, a tattoo artist and small business owner, offered free tattoos to anybody who was ready to represent the new found Trump movement. People got tattoos of "Make America Great Again"; tattoos of Trump's face on their bodies; tattoos of "The Donald" and any other saying they could think of to represent Trump, including "Take Our Country Back." Chris Cox started a bikers club named Bikers for Trump. They would chant, "We want our country back!" while riding down the road. Trump had made them believe he would take the country in a new direction and as a result his movement continued to grow. Minister Farrakhan warned, "Trump is giving white people hope that they can put black people back "in their place." And when Trump says he wants to make America great again, he used racially coded language that really meant he wanted to make America white again.

"What amazes a lot of people is that I'm sitting in an apartment the likes of which nobody has ever seen," The President of the United States said, smiling. "And yet I represent the workers of the world," he tells "Time" magazine. "I'm representing them and they love me and I love them."

*"Use selective honesty and generosity
to disarm your victims."*

— *Robert Greene*

"Play to people's fantasies."

— *Robert Greene*

Farrakhan Talks More

"Now look at Mr. Trump. He is giving the common white people hope that they can be superior again. Donald Trump is causing white people to say, "I'm sick and tired of turning on my television and seeing our former slaves talking to us like they are our bosses!" Once we put our brother in office, we've had to suffer the past eight years of being in the White House because white folks thought we were getting "uppity." So at every turn they've been trying to put blacks—the black man and woman—"back in their place." That's what "stop and frisk" is all about. That's what shooting down blacks for no cause is all about. That's what lead in drinking water is all about. That's what taking vaccinations when you don't need them is all about!

In 2016 they found Trump to be such a liar that they set up a website to track his lies. He lied about the loan his father gave him. He lied about his bankruptcies, his federal financial disclosure forms, about his endorsements and about Obama's birth certificate. He also lied about seeing thousands of Arabs in New Jersey celebrating the tragedy of 9-1-1; about paying his taxes, about Mexicans, about Muslims, about his casinos, about money from donors and about his wonderful university...The news magazine "Politico" tracked him over five hours of remarks and found that he averaged about one lie every three minutes and fifteen seconds. Therefore, in five days he lied 87 times. But his supporters didn't care. They allowed Trump to lie his way to the presidency. Trump believed it didn't matter what he said or did. He believed his supporters were extremely loyal. And they were.

American   Money   Publishing

WE PUBLISH THE REALIST BOOKS

Chapter Fourteen

Trump Effect

After Trump told America he no longer wanted immigrants coming to the United States, he opened a door for others to also reveal how they felt about immigrants coming into their countries. Canada has emerged as one of the countries where there has to be a limit. "Prime Minister Justin Trudeau is forcing immigration down Canadian's throats," Margaret Wente said. "Don't get me wrong. Canada is one of the most successful immigrant-friendly countries on earth, and we are justifiably proud of that. But there is a limit." Canada has accepted 320,932 immigrants and refugees in 2016; one-third more immigrants than in 2015.

People in Canada are starting to believe that accepting immigrants need to pass a "Canadian values test" before they can live in Canada. They also feel that minorities who are already living there need to do more to fit in. Some of the critics feel that all those feelings have emerged from the rhetoric of Donald Trump and it has inspired Canadians to unleash how they have always felt about their inner racism. However, Prime Minister Trudeau believes that immigration will revive the fortunes of flagging towns. But Margaret Wente said, "Immigrants rarely move to the boondocks and start businesses. No, they move to the cities where the jobs are and compete with the rest of us for housing and services.

Trudeau talks about what Canada must do for them but not what they must do for Canada. "If his liberal party continues to ignore the genuine concerns of ordinary voters, it is asking for a backlash." Trump is not alone in feeling that immigrants need to go back to wherever they came from. Many people feel the same way, including Europe and Canada, and silently many other people and countries.

*"He was unafraid to say what many other
leaders wanted to say."*
— *Patterson*

White Supremacist Supporter

One man couldn't believe his luck. Finally, someone had come along and was talking his language. His name is William Johnson and he was thrilled by the rise of Donald Trump. He is the head of the American Freedom Party and did not hide the fact that he is a white nationalist, who has spent the past 30 years on the border of American politics; who promotes the political interests of the white race and the deportation of all HISPANICS, ASIANS, JEWS and BLACKS. But with Trump rising to the title of nominee for the Republican Party, Johnson stated, "My extremist views are no longer beyond pale." He recalled that for many years when he would express how he felt, other people would call him names like "hatemonger," or "Nazi" or "Hitler." Now, after the rise of Trump, they're saying, "Oh, you're like Donald Trump." The white supremacist today is a 61-year old corporate lawyer who lives on a 67-acre ranch in Los Angeles who rushed to sign-up and become one of Trump's delegates in the Republican Presidential Primary in California.

"The white race is dying out in America and Europe because we are afraid to be called a racist."

— *William Johnson*

Changing the Rules

There is no reason to believe that Trump stands for anything other than a personal hunger to expand his wealth and power. He will change position on a political issue faster than a blink of an eye. He's committed every sin in the book and still Christian conservatives stand by him. He's guilty of greed, lust, adultery, spite and wrath. Whatever his intentions, it's clear that it's a plot to undermine religion by subordinating it to politics. Trump had people so off-base that Republicans were confused as to what candidate they should back. They had to consider their reputations and what their next moves should be when preparing to answer the crucial questions they would face when voters asked what their positions were after Trump launched into his inflamed earth rampage. It included his unbridled late night Twitter rants in which he blasted everybody who's against him—from Megyn Kelly to a former Miss Universe to the family of a fallen Muslim-American soldier. But his supporters would shrug off his rhetoric, calling it showmanship honed by his years as a TV star from the show "The Apprentice." They would say there are two Trumps:

the private Trump who was far more reasonable, charming and generous. And then there was the Trump who didn't care what the world thought of him. If anything was bad, he would deny it. If it was unusual, he would use it to his advantage.

The results on November 8th would prove that Trump had not only violated the rules, he had changed them to work in his favor. There were now new rules and only Trump had the "third eye" to see them. "Not having a traditional operation hurt him less than people thought it would. And in this social media age, saying outrageous things may not really be a disadvantage," analyst Van Jones said. Trump knew what he was doing while the rest of the world slept.

"Conceal your intentions."
— *Robert Greene*

Trump's Threat

Trump spared nobody who attacked him, including the media. When women began to emerge from the underground with allegations of sexual assaults by Donald, he did not only go after the women, he threatened to go after the "New York

Times" for printing them. "Donald Trump's threat to sue the 'New York Times' is yet another sign of his dangerously authoritarian impulses," said Eric Boehm. Trump became furious after reading the disturbing information published by the Times. The story reported that two women accused Trump of inappropriately touching them without their consent. At least 10 women have come forward since Trump claimed he never sexually assaulted the women. However, Jessica Leeds who sat next to Trump on a flight had a very interesting story to tell about him. She stated he lifted his armrest and put his hand on her breasts and attempted to rub them. He also tried to put a hand underneath her shirt. "He was like an octopus," his accuser said. "His hands were everywhere." After he didn't stop, she moved to the back of the plane.

On another occasion Trump and his wife, Melania, were being interviewed by "People" magazine. The interviewer was Natasha Stoynoff and they were at Trump's Mar-a-lago estate. When his wife—who was pregnant with their son Barron—left the room, it was reported that Trump shut the door, pushed Stoynoff up against the wall and began kissing her in the mouth. "We're going to have an affair, I'm telling you," he told her while

Melania was right upstairs. Trump decided he would sue "The New York Times" for publishing the women's accounts of what happened. He had his lawyers write a letter which contained a warning to the magazine that Trump would file a lawsuit against them if they didn't retract the story.

But the threat had no effect on the Times who were not afraid and their lawyers fired back, challenging Trump to try and sue. "You've already ruined your own reputation and legally you have no case," they wrote back. "He thinks he should be off limits for investigations by the media into behavior he's bragged about and admitted to doing. In fact, this is the same Trump who has said he'd like to open the libel laws to make it easier for public figures like him to sue the media for opinion articles and news stories he deems 'unfair'. Imagine what a President Trump might do with federal prosecutors to do his bidding rather than using personal attorneys. We are perilously close to sending to the White House a man who cannot—or will not—respect basic rights held by the people of the country he wishes to lead," "The New York Times" lawyers said.

Chapter Fifteen

Still Rising

It was 1990 and Trump had taken a one million dollar loan from his father and then catapulted to billionaire status. He became Manhattan's real estate mogul by raising the value of real estate in New York. He had become a celebrity in his own right, especially after it was discovered he had been having an affair with beauty queen-model Marla Maples. He would end up divorcing his first wife, Ivana, and it dominated the New York City tabloids. After several months of front-page headlines in papers and magazines Ivana decided to ship the children to boarding school to protect them from the media. And while Trump was going through the divorce, not only was he losing Ivana but he was losing his fortune.

By the time Donald finally proposed to Marla in 1993, Trump was flat broke. He had to file for bankruptcy on four of his businesses. He tried to borrow his way out of debt but no banks would deal with him. But as time passed the banks realized they needed Trump. He would develop a mastermind of an idea: license the name "Trump." When people would see the name "Trump" on large buildings, it automatically gave the building prestige. Running with that idea, Trump was on his way back to the top. Trump and Maples had a daughter, Tiffany, which probably helped him make up his mind to go ahead and get married. So in 1993 he and Marla married.

Being a winner wasn't just something Donald exhibited, it was inside of him and he proved it to himself and the world by bouncing back. He negotiated with the banks to lower his debts in the wake of his bankruptcies and was able to report a loss of nearly one billion in taxes. That clever move allowed him to avoid paying income taxes for the next 18 years. Trump knew how to think outside the box and he constantly thought of ways to get out of debt and to get back on top. He was the infamous Donald J. Trump and he refused to lose. His sister said, "He always wins."

"When people told him it was impossible for a boy from Queens to go to
Manhattan and take on developers in the big city, rather than give up,
he changed the skyline of New York."

— Donald Trump, Jr.

Boldness

Trump entered the race for President with boldness. When he reached his sixties he started to think more about the Presidency of the United States. He felt he was running out of time. He'd already given over $700,000 thousand dollars to Democrats and in 2012 he endorsed Mitt Romney. But those he backed did not become Presidents. So Trump was finally ready to give up his good life and do what he could to make America great again. He started to believe that he was the only one who could do it. Although he had considered running for President and had mentioned it to Oprah and the media when he was younger, he knew he was unsure and it would have been foolish to attempt it which is why he first tried to back other candidates. He knew with the doubts he had he could not run effectively; and if he was not 100% ready he would make mistakes and fail.

He knew if he ran timid, it would be dangerous so he had to make sure he was ready.

In 2015 he felt he was ready and announced he was running for President of the United States. When asked if he thought he could really win he replied, "I don't run races I don't think I can win. I always win." He decided he would run and he would run his way; a way that had never been used before. He knew it would be abnormal but he would enter the race with boldness. Using a strategy of boldness he knew his mistakes would be overlooked because they would be committed with audacity and would easily be corrected with more audacity. The nation was already secretly divided and there was a group of people who felt neglected and would understand him, believing that he understood them and they would look to him as their Savior. Everybody eventually admire the bold; no one honors a scared man who appears intimidated. Hesitation puts obstacles in your path but boldness eliminates them. If Trump had entered the race with less than total confidence, he would have set obstacles in his path. And when challenged on political issues, he would've felt timid, confused and started to believe he was out of his league.

But his boldness threw everyone off-guard. Instead of being confused, he confused his opponents which made him seem bigger than life. Any timidity faded into the shadows but the bold, like Trump, drew attention. He knew a secret that his opponents apparently did not: When a man draws attention, he also draws power. That's why every time he made an offensive attack his fame and power grew, capturing new and more supporters. His supporters were at the point where they would wait in anticipation for his next outrageous attack against an opponent or anyone who opposed him. Trump is a master at the art of audacity just as he bills himself as the master of the art of the deal. When he said he would renegotiate trade deals in America with other countries it was believable because the world knows that's what he had perfected. He is the ultimate deal-maker. There is no man or woman who is perfect so we all have weaknesses. But when you enter a venture with boldness it has the magical effect of making your weaknesses appear invisible. Just like with con artists they know how to sell a lie. But they also know that the bolder the lie, the more convincing it will become. It's the audacity of his intentions that gives his words more credibility. Trump knew this as well.

People couldn't believe the things that he was saying. Everything he said sounded unbelievable. No one had ever come out publicly and made vulgar statements like Trump did. People thought he was insane. Most people want to avoid tension and conflict and be liked and loved by everyone. And some people will plot on a bold action but rarely will they act on it. They're scared, unsure and terrified of the consequences, more concerned with how others would think of them. No one wants to be viewed as the man or woman who stirs up trouble. They don't want to deal with the hostility they might face. Plus, people fear going beyond their comfort zones. Boldness directs attention outward and keeps the illusion alive. It has the power to never induce awkwardness or embarrassment in the person. Those who are bold are usually admired; people want to be around them. They are the types that take control and can lead other people, creating a movement. Donald Trump said he was not running a campaign but "a movement."

People flock to those who are self-confident about their ability to be themselves without caring how they are perceived. Not all people are born with boldness but when they are they will stand out amongst the crowd or even within the world. When you enter into an action boldly there is no limit to what you might do, might say or might ask for. At first, it might seem foolish to the listener or your opponent but they will soon realize that it took guts to do what was done or said. Being bold makes people stop and pay attention when it's abnormal or different. It's boldness! It comes with both applause and ridicule but it accomplishes what needs to be done. Donald J. Trump is now the President of the United States because he was not timid, he was not a follower and he created his own path.

"Enter action with boldness" — Law #28
— Robert Greene

Chapter Sixteen

Trump or WW3

VOTE TRUMP OR ITS WORLD WARIII warned an extremist ally of President Vladimir Putin, the President of Russia. It has been rumored that Russia had given its input into who would be the President of the United States which included hacking and finding Hillary Clinton's emails which indicated wrongdoings. There have been warnings that America needs to vote for Donald Trump or face nuclear devastation. Vladimir Zhirinovsky, leader of Russia's Ultranationalist Liberal Democratic Party said, "If they vote for Hillary its war." He continued with, "It will be a short movie. There will be Hiroshima's and Nagasaki's everywhere." Although Americans possibly paid no attention to Zhirinovsky who is highly recognized for his agitating, anti-Muslim and grandiloquent language and amusingly compares himself to Trump. He has run for President in every election since the destruction of the Soviet Union and has yet to win.

Zhirinovsky has become recognized as a spokesperson for Vladimir Putin and was recently honored by the Kremlin. It is not beneath him to throw out radical ideas to see how people will react to them. Whether people reacted or not, no one knows. But America does believe that Russia's President, Vladimir Putin, wanted Donald Trump to become President of the United States. This was scary because Americans think Putin is a murderer and a very bad man who has a lot of power.

"Every time I did something they'd say,
'Oh, he did that because of Russia.'
They tried to make it that because...
they tried to build up my relationship
to Russia which is really nonexistent
other than I think I will get along with
Vladimir Putin and I think we're going to...
I think getting along with
Russia's a good thing, not a bad thing."
— Donald Trump

One thing that is certain in Trump's inflammable and increasingly unrestrained campaign, Trump has, by one count, belittled almost 300 people, places or things. He has shown disdain to anybody or anything that got in his way or upset him. He has attacked Mexicans and immigrants, Fox News anchor Megyn Kelly, Muslims and Belgians, China and Iowans, House Speaker Paul Ryan, Republican Senator John McCain, German Chancellor Angela Merkel, "The New York Times," Dallas Maverick's NBA owner Mark Cuban, Pope Francis, Hillary and Bill Clinton, his sexual assault women accusers, people with mental issues, refugees and even late night TV talk show hosts. But Trump has never said anything bad about Vladimir Putin. "Russia's remorseless, autocratic, murderer Vladimir Putin, for some very odd and confusing reason, has only been defended by Donald Trump."

"Any friend of mine, we share the same enemy."
— *Patterson*

Continue to Rise

Trump and Maples appeared to be a beautiful couple but the marriage would not last too long.

It actually came to an end right before the deadline of the prenuptial agreement. It was rumored that if the marriage didn't last a certain amount of years, Marla Maples would walk away with a couple of millions which it's believed to have been the outcome. His divorce was finalized in 1999 and Trump had already been seeing Slovenian model Melania Knauss who he would eventually marry and father a son, Barron Trump. They would have a fairytale wedding in 2005 and conceive Barron a year later. Trump would also start his journey to becoming a real estate mogul and celebrity by cultivating a public persona. He would give cameos, playing himself in movies and on TV. He was also becoming more recognized as Trump the billionaire who made it big from real estate.

He began directing the Miss Universe pageant where he was around the most beautiful women in the world. His image as Donald Trump began to become bigger-than-life. Hollywood as well as TV networks realized that he was marketable. So in 2004, Trump launched his first TV show, "The Apprentice," and Donald Trump's name became a household word. The show was a success for over a decade with Trump playing himself and saying the phrase that would become famous, "You're fired!"

Trump once said that he would run for President but the idea of it happening was laughable. He was already living the dream life plus, he was not presidential material. But through the show "The Apprentice" the entire country now knew who he was. When approached about a new season for the show, Trump declined. He was going to pursue his old dream of the presidency. He decided "The Apprentice" would have a spinoff with a new show titled "The Celebrity Apprentice" with Arnold Schwarzenegger (the Terminator) as host.

"The show must go on."

— *Patterson*

Rearranged the Furniture

Hitler would send his soldiers to all the places and homes of the Jews and Germans in power and have them arrested. He would put them in jail and strip them of their authority. After they were all captured, Hitler gained control of the military. Under Hitler over six million people would be arrested, mutilated and/or murdered. Hundreds of thousands of young men from several nations would fight, get injured and /or be killed. The historians of the military would never forget the pain, the battle and the terrible and horrible memory of it all. There would be a series of moves and countermoves structured like a chess game by men in powerful positions.

There were omnipotent generals with different stripes, sitting in hidden headquarters and giving orders. They wear different uniforms and have a high rank, but their backgrounds and training are the same. They have the same maps and the same ideals. For them, to earn the right of power from their unseen opponent is not so personal. But it is completely different for the soldier who fights on the soil. "I like war," Trump said but his feet would never stand on the dirt of the terrain. He even skipped out on war in his latter teen years when he chose to get an education. When he was young Trump was very aware of Hitler and of the wars because he lived in that time. He doesn't know the pain of soldiers on the ground. But that is not what's important to him. What's important to him is to make America great again. As long as he does that, it doesn't matter how many people will suffer and die. Trump is not a soldier, he is a king. And kings don't fight the battle, but they are the ones who are remembered. Trump only cares about his personal battle of will; to outsmart his enemy with moral strength and tactical ingenuity.

But war for the people equals tragedy, just as it does for the soldiers. It is a day-to-day life of drama, disaster, bloodshed and death. Soldiers' orders are simple: attack, capture and if necessary—die. There are no in-betweens. Defend to the last man and the last bullet. Trump wants to go back to the ways of Hitler. A man once wrote, "It is as great a mistake to return to the old battlefield as it is to revisit the place of your honeymoon or the home you grew up in. For years you have owned them in your memory. When you go back, you find the occupants have rearranged the furniture."

Chapter Seventeen

4th Grade Vocabulary

"I know words. I have the best words," Donald Trump once bragged. But it doesn't appear as if he knows big words. Trump does not seem to have an extensive vocabulary. While his opponents were using 6th to 10th grade level words, Trump was annihilating them during the debates with 4th grade level language. His vocabulary was that of a 4th grader, but apparently he said all the right things. "Hillary hurt us. She completely forgot about us. That's why we voted for Trump," a former Democratic oil miner said. Trump didn't want to sound highly educated. He wanted to sound like the voters who lacked education. That's why he was such a success when it counted. He played the role of an uneducated politician, a regular person who gave unrehearsed speeches. His unsavory attacks on Jeb Bush, Marco Rubio, Ben Carson and whoever he felt needed slashing jump-started him straight to the nomination.

It was puzzling. Trump gave the impression he was a joke and not to be taken seriously. He did things like a man who didn't even want to win. It's clear that he's not much of a reader. It is rumored that he doesn't read his own books and would not waste a minute of his time reading other books. He also expressed that he refuse to read other people's words. It is said that the only time Trump has read something is when he read his father's eulogy at his funeral. "Those are the only prepared remarks he's ever delivered, to my knowledge, before now," biographer Wayne Barrett said. "He talks all the time about how he doesn't want to bore his audience. He's more worried about boring himself."

But he's never boring because he can never stay focused on a subject longer than six minutes. He will bring up an issue without ever offering a solution. "We're going to be great," he would say then pretend to act like he cares about blacks just to get their votes. "Nearly four in ten African-American children live in poverty and 58% of African-American youth are not working! More than 2,700 black and brown-skinned people have been shot in Chicago this year alone!" Trump doesn't explain why it's happening or what's his plan to fix it? He just talks and talks so he doesn't become bored. His audience doesn't care about blacks but they still look confused. They're not sure when to clap or when to get excited. He confuses black and Latinos who listens on TV or radio when he finished a civil rights speech with, "African-American citizens and Latino citizens will have the time of their lives," he promised if he becomes President. That statement left everybody scratching their head.

> *"Play a sucker to catch a sucker seems*
> *dumber than your mark."*
>
> — *Robert Greene*

Construction

"I ordered the immediate building of our fortifications in the west," Hitler announced as he addressed over 250 thousand people at a rally in Nuremburg. It would be the first time he would reveal the secret about the construction of The Great Wall. He would have damn near a million citizens on the border with France. "I can assure that since May 28th the most giant fortification work of all time has been constructed." The West Wall, which Hitler continually boasted about, was totally different from the Maginot Line. The Maginot Line was basically a thin line of forts. However, the Maginot Line was built to never be brought down. It was built with depth; two miles and a half of hundreds of collective supporting concrete emplacements, observation and command post. It was connected by concrete roads with military shelters and bunkers.

The Maginot Line was considered a prestige item with air conditioning, underground cinemas, hospitals, suntan parlors and more. But the West Wall was basically Germanic—hard, lean and spartan.

The great undertaking began in May of 1938. Hitler had ordered the wall to be built within 18 months. The man he put in charge was just an engineer and well-liked by Hitler. He was a German who went by the name of Todt. He was good and rallied up huge resources in free and very low-cost labor. It wasn't hard because Germany was barely recovering from a Depression. He utilized the Reichsarbeitsdienst (RAD), the Nazi labor force which every boy and girl had to participate in the moment they turned 17. They would have to work for free for six months. Todt used free labor to dig the foundation and the anti-tank traps. People needed money and The Wall provided several jobs: bricklayers, engineers and carpenters who were happy to take the jobs even if they didn't agree with the building of The Wall.

In the end, after all the free labor and help had been hired, there would be 100,000 military engineers, 350,000 men—who were a part of Todt's outfit he called Organization Todt—and thousands of the RAD workers. In the first 15 months, eight million tons of cement was used. They also used over a million tons of steel and iron and almost a million tons of wood. They built 14,000 bunkers and pillboxes. They were in a 400-mile line, 35 per mile at a cost of 3.5 marks. The Wall was the greatest construction program undertaken in Germany's history.

The bunkers were built 20 to 21 feet wide and as high as 18 feet with a depth of 42 feet. The roofs and walls were fortified with up to concrete as thick as nine feet. Most of the structure was built deep into the ground and contained web-bottomed beds, synchronized in tiers to sleep 14-man troops. The majority of the bunkers were equipped with two firing holes and the way the pillboxes were situated in clusters it allowed the guns, machine guns and cannons to cover any intruders. The Wall would wind its way through Germany like a deadly snake waiting to strike. We can only imagine that this is the same vision Donald Trump has.

Slayed the Legacy

It has been said that "a man must avoid stepping into a great man's shoes." Frederick Trump was considered a great man to people in real estate and to his family. Donald was once asked did he try to outdo his father. "No, I don't think so," he responded. He was asked that because for his first project he built a high-rise skyscraper while his father only built houses. But an old saying goes, "What happens first always appear better and more original than what comes afterwards." If you have a famous parent or succeed beyond a great person, you will have to accomplish double their achievements to outshine them. Do not get lost in their shadow or stuck in a past not of your own making. You must establish your own name and identity by changing course. Slay the overbearing father, dismantle his legacy and gain power by shining in your new identity. That's the 41st law of *The 48 Laws of Power* and Trump must have known about the law because he definitely slayed his father's legacy and created his own for his children to try and conquer.

Trump created an empire so large that when people think of or hear the name Trump, they think of Donald J. Trump. He represents an extremely uncommon type in history or in today's times. He's the son of a powerful and successful man who managed to take the family empire to heights it had never seen or imagined. He surpassed his father in glory, fame, money and power. Fred Trump was never a billionaire. But Donald J. Trump became a billionaire twice. This kind of success is uncommon for a son because the father amasses his fortune and kingdom and usually he begins with little or nothing, creating a desperate urge which impels him to succeed. He has nothing to lose by being cunning and impetuous and has no famous father to compete against. This kind of man has reason to believe in himself; to believe that his way of doing things is the best because after all, it worked for him. And once a powerful man like that has a son, he can become domineering and oppressive; imposing his lessons onto his son who is starting off in life in totally different circumstances from those his father began in. Instead of allowing the son to advance in a new direction, the father will try to make him follow in his footsteps, perhaps secretly hoping the son will fail or using the son to keep the legacy alive and grow the business. Fathers can have a tendency to envy their sons' youth and vigor. After all, their desire is to control and dominate. The sons of such men tend to become cowardly and cautious, terrified of losing what their fathers have accomplished.

The son will never step out of his father's shadow unless he adopts a ruthless strategy of doing things his own way. By dismantling the past, creating your own kingdom and putting the father in the shadows instead of letting him do it to you. If you cannot materially start from ground zero, it would be foolish to renounce an inheritance. But you can at least begin from ground zero, psychologically, by throwing off the weight of the past and charting a new direction. That is the reason Trump is so successful, although he did follow in his father's footsteps with real estate. But he took it in a different direction. It was more risky, more of a challenge and would generate more money. The direction Donald Trump took put him in an entirely different league than his father. And with his father's loan of a million dollars, there was no fear of losing all that his father had gained.

Trump completely outshone his father and literally inherited the name, Trump. He made the family's name bigger than life. It will still be remembered a thousand years after his death. Just like Alexander the Great, he instinctively recognized that the privileges of birth can be impediments to power. Be merciless with the past, not only your father's and his father's but your own earlier achievements. Only the weak rest on their laurels and dote on past triumphs. In the game of power there is never time to rest. Never let yourself be seen as following your predecessor's path. If you do you will never surpass him. You must physically demonstrate your difference by establishing a style and symbolism which sets you apart.

"Accomplish double their achievement."

Robert Greene

AMP

American   Money   Publishing

WE PUBLISH THE REALIST BOOKS

Chapter Eighteen

Billionaire Supporter

Although Trump bragged that he was rich and he needed no one else's money because he couldn't be bought out, he had no problem ACCEPTING TECH BILLIONAIRE PETER THIEL'S 1.25 MILLION TO AID TRUMP'S CANDIDACY. Peter Thiel defended his support of Donald Trump after receiving strong criticism from Washington and the Silicon Valley elites. "What Donald Trump represents isn't crazy and it's not going away," Thiel said, although he did believe that Donald Trump's groping of women was clearly offensive and inappropriate, he would not judge Trump by his flaws on Election Day. "We're voting for Trump because we judge the leadership of our country," Thiel said. "This judgment has certainly been hard to accept for Silicon Valley where many people have learned not to dissent from the coastal bubble," he added. Thiel stuck by his decision even though some people in the tech world have called for the billionaire to be dropped from the board of the social network giant Facebook and California Y combinatory over donations.

Thiel made his fortune by co-founding PayPal and said the pushback has not affected his business dealings in any meaningful way. "Trump gets the big things right such as understanding that free trade has not worked out well for all of America. Also, voters have grown tired of 15 years of overseas conflicts." For those reasons Thiel placed his support behind Trump. That support created the most quarrelsome debate in Silicon Valley. The early Facebook investor was always considered an outsider among the other tech elites because of his strange, unrestricted liberal outlook. Now, they feel he went too far which has caused a division amongst them. They even considered banishing him while other firms have thought about cutting ties with him. They feel if they deal with Thiel, the tech giants are approving Trump's sexist activities and racist character which might cast a reflection on them—their tech boardrooms are predominantly all white men. However, Facebook giant Mark

Zuckerberg defends Thiel. "It's wrong to purge someone for his political beliefs; both sides have valid points. Thiel's position shouldn't make him immune from criticism and Silicon Valley's immense wealth and political power suggests its leaders' values matter deeply." But according to "The Week" there's a difference between denouncing Thiel and pressuring everyone who works with him to exit him out. But Donald Trump has been proven to divide people from families all the way up the ladder to giant tech billionaires.

"It's wrong to purge a man for his political beliefs."
— *Mark Zuckerberg*

Re-creation of Trump

Donald Trump's father's business was doing extremely well. In fact, so good that Donald and his brothers and sisters were living "high off the hog." All of them grew up in an environment of privilege. They lived in a 23 room mansion located in Queens, New York in the exclusive neighborhood of Jamaica Estates. They were driven to and from a private school by a chauffeur in a limousine every day. Trump was raised among money and he was raised to make more of it. They were all raised to be winners and the best at whatever they did. His sister Maryanne Trump became a federal judge and she is very good at what she does with major power and influence. Donald started out badly and was not always on his best behavior at school. "As an adolescent I was mostly interested in mischief," Donald admitted. So at the age of 13 his father sent him to the New York Military Academy in Cornwall-on-Hudson, New York.

Trump's leadership skills began to develop and he became a student leader at the all-boys military school. He was charming, he knew the right words to say and he knew how to play on people's generosity. Therefore, he became the love of his classmates. In a yearbook poll they voted him "ladies man." Even as a teenager he had been winning over people's votes. He realized while in that all-boys school that he had to re-create himself—and he did.

*"Become the master of your own image —
re-create yourself."*
— *Robert Greene*

He began to take life more seriously. He began to understand his position and realized education was power. He would learn that being decisive about what you wanted and wanted to do in life would serve him better than being stupid and not taking life seriously. There was no future in it. Therefore, he stepped up his game and started taking life more seriously which resulted in him making power moves. He hasn't look back.

Rigged

Trump would attack anything or anyone that impeded something he'd set his eyes on or wanted to become. "The election is being rigged!" Trump shouted to his supporters after sliding in the polls. He'd gone on a Tweet rampage and was telling his supporters at his rallies, "The election is being stolen from me through large-scale voter fraud," he told them. He said it was all being implemented through biased media coverage from CNN, conspiracy between international banks and United States elites who'd rather see Clinton as the President and not him. They wanted Clinton because Trump said she would enrich her donors and abrade U.S. sovereignty. So he started throwing out warnings. "Watch your polling booths, especially in the inner-city areas," he told his supporters. Then election officials started warning him to stop his rhetoric and accusations.

What Trump was doing was unprecedented and it began to lead to racial altercations, confrontations, and in some cases, violent attacks at polling stations. But Trump didn't care. He attacked the American polling system like it was an imminent enemy. President Obama told Trump, "Quit whining before the game's even over!" Then a Politico poll stated that at least 73% of Republicans believed the election could be rigged with fraud, introducing skepticism into their belief in American polls. Trump and his clan of supporters started going crazy. They were willing to kill if Trump didn't win. "We are ready to take arms if Trump loses!" a supporter yelled out. "Pitchforks and torches time," David Clark, a Milwaukee Sheriff sinisterly Tweeted. "Clinton should be in prison or shot!"

They were ready for outright war over Trump. He was belittling America by implying the U.S. elections were illegitimate. "Trump's conspiracy theory is complete and utter bunk," the Nationalreview.com said. The country should know that whoever wins, it will be as a result of being chosen by the American electorate. It is not simple for an election to be rigged. It's controlled by local officials in 50 different states and each vote is deeply scrutinized by officials of each party with independent monitors. But Trump still doesn't trust the system and is not backing down, stating that if he loses it is because the system is RIGGED.

"Use distractions to take away attention from your faults."

— *Patterson*

Chapter Nineteen

Assassination Plot

During one of Trump's campaign rallies in Las Vegas, one of Trump's enemies tried to take his life. He had been plotting to murder the man he'd grown to hate for over a year. There's no telling how many men and women wanted to assassinate the real estate mogul. Now, one has been arrested for attempted murder by the name of Michael Steven Sanford. He is a British man who—by the age of 20—was living in the U.S. illegally after his visa expired. While Trump was giving a speech about how great of a guy he was and how he would make America great again, Michael Sanford slowly walked up to a police officer. His mind was probably racing and his heart pumping hard. He hated Trump and he wanted him dead. He had bought a ticket to the next rally in the event he chickened out of his plans in Vegas. But so far it looked as if he was going to do it.

He kept his eyes on the officer's gun as everything seemed to move in slow motion. "Do it. Do it. Don't think. Don't hesitate. Just do it," his inner voice told him over and over and over again. "Just do it," he told himself as he got closer and closer. He reached out and tried to grab the policeman's gun but the officer reacted quickly and prevented Sanford from snatching the gun and was able to take him down. "Hey! Hey! You're hurting me!" Sanford screamed while he was being subdued and handcuffed. He was quickly detained by security and was hauled off to jail where he was charged with committing a violent act. Trump literally dodged a bullet that day but the question is, will he be just as lucky the next time? Because there is no doubt that if Trump keeps on making new enemies, the next one might be better prepared.

The Director

As a rule, the FBI is usually hush-hush about information and evidence on a case. FBI Director James Comey had always been known as less than tight-lipped. As he told the world, under oath on Capitol Hill, about the Hillary Clinton email investigation, he decided to tell the world about his upbringing as well. "I was raised by great parents who taught me you can't care what other people think about you," he said, trying to explain his appearance and the fact that he found no evidence against Hillary. "In my business I have to and deeply do...that people have confidence that the system's not fixed against blacks, for rich people, for powerful people." He wanted to make it clear that he was not biased and that the FBI was fair. They had chosen—based on his authority and recommendation—not to charge Hillary Clinton. Because of that decision, Comey would have some rough months to follow.

Donald Trump traveled all around the country condemning Comey's decision not to indict Hillary. He suggested it was a crooked effort at a cover up. He felt the system was rigged if Hillary Clinton was allowed to run for President. But the FBI rolled over and the Department of Justice rolled over. So Trump continued to speak, ranting and fulminating everyday on TV that if it had been anybody else besides a Clinton they would be in jail. He called her "crooked Hillary" and implied she had Director Comey and the FBI in her back pocket.

However, 10 days before the election, with Trump behind in the polls, Comey plunged back into the election with devastating news that would cripple Hillary's campaign. He alerted Congress that more emails had been discovered that were possibly damaging evidence to the Clinton investigation. He did this although he had no idea if the newly discovered evidence showed any wrongdoing. His action reopened the investigation and it was announced to the world through a letter to Congress which became breaking news. This would be a serious blow to Clinton's campaign and public image. Democrats were furious and they reacted in fury. They demanded an explanation to show some type of proof that the evidence was damaging. "It's plenty strange to put something out there like that with such little information right before an election. In fact, it's not just strange, it's unprecedented and it's deeply troubling," Hillary Clinton said.

Hillary had a good lead but her advantage began to diminish after Comey's announcement. So a rumor surfaced that Director James Comey's words would swing the election in Trump's favor. However, there are rules that are supposed to prevent such a disaster. Law is supposed to have order and there are guidelines in the Justice Department to protect itself from political interference. But allegations of political interference echoed throughout the country when the FBI implied it had evidence against Hillary Clinton. They spoke on a case that eventually ended without any charges. But this wasn't anything new to Comey. He knew that the rules were not designed to withstand the formidable pressures of the moment: a governing city at war with itself; a nation flooded in bottomless conspiracy theories; and people in charge who compromise their impartiality.

Bill Clinton, ironically, boarded Attorney General Loretta Lynch's plane on an airport tarmac for a personal visit. This action was appalling to Trump and aroused his suspicions that the Clinton's were above the law. Eventually, that decision forced Loretta Lynch to agree to take Comey's recommendations in the investigation. President Obama had his say on the situation as well. In defense of his legacy, he prejudged the investigation, saying publically in 2015, "Hillary Clinton did not endanger national security." Yet, a flurry of political forces bonded to the email scandal and the Director's role in it believed it put him in an untenable position, especially if Clinton had won the election and became the United States President. It was terribly bad timing and it left a bad taste in the mouths of Democrats and the Clintons. "If you are President-elect Clinton, how do you put this behind you, particularly if this entire matter is still pending when you take office?" asked Ron Hosko, the former FBI Assistant Director and head of the Bureau's Criminal Investigation Division. "How can you have an effective relationship if every time you are in the same room together this shadow looms? This is a perilous path that he's on. I think he had to go into this with eyes wide open; I don't think he took this lightly."

It looked like the Clintons didn't have as much power as Trump because once he started on his rampage about Comey's first decision not to charge Hillary Clinton, Comey reentered the election with a new decision. And this time it was like the atomic bomb of Hiroshima being dropped on Hillary Clinton. And it would eventually blow her out of the water. Justin Byerly of Asheville, North Carolina said his decision was difficult. "Until 11 days ago I was for Hillary," he said, "then the emails happened."

Farrakhan Keeps Talking

You don't know when your life is hanging in the balance; and who you vote for is critical to SAVING YOUR LIFE and the lives of your people. Let's prove a point Elijah Muhammad was making. "If the present Party [Democratic] remains in office, you know the answer. If the Republican Party takes over, you should know the answer." THERE WILL BE A LULL BEFORE THE STORM. The storm can be delayed, but every hour and day that it is delayed is to the black man's benefit. "But you can't put the storm off forever. That's the point. It's coming. So one of the candidates will delay it but nobody can turn away a storm because there is nothing in their political platforms that will stop the storm from coming." Now what should be their platform to stop the storm? And most importantly, what is "the storm?" Understand that God is in the picture now. America is under divine judgment. This will increase now because I'm standing in the place of the Messenger—the Messiah—and my job is to warn you and then get out of the way.

CLINTON VS. TRUMP: These lying wonders are actors in a scheme controlled by a smart, crooked Satan. The devil is producing what is called "lying wonders." When Hillary lost to Barack in 2008, she and her husband were both against Barack. Do blacks remember when Mr. Clinton said, "Gee, just a few years ago this man would've been serving us coffee?" And then Barack appoints her as his Secretary of State. But in her mind, all the time she is "there," every move she makes is with the thought that in "four years" or "eight years" she would become the President of the United States. She did things as Secretary of State that would show her prowess in international theaters. She visited 112 countries and she was a policy maker; then along came Osama Bin Laden. But the biggest thing she did was impress upon the President that, "We have to stop Muammar Gaddafi." And when he was dead, her words were:

"We came, we saw, he's dead."
— Hillary Clinton

Donald J. Tump

Like A King

When Trump had finally completed military school he had a different outlook about himself. His mischievous ways had evaporated and his re-creation as a man of leadership had emerged. He ended up enrolling in Fordham University in New York City. But after two short years he made the decision to transfer to the University of Pennsylvania's prestigious Wharton School. His father wanted him to have the best education possible and Trump would do the same for his children. The Trump family realized that having the best education was the secret to becoming the best in whatever field you chose to work in. Trump began to make preparations for his career and of course he decided to study real estate. He would earn a Bachelor degree in economics.

After he obtained his degree, he immediately plunged into the family business and joined the Trump Management Corporation. The business was well-established in developing and maintaining low and middle income housing. He was intrigued by his father's work ethics and would imitate his style of management. He caught on fast and it appeared easy for him; it was obvious he was a natural in the field of real estate. And in a few years he surpassed his brother, Freddy, and would become his father's successor at the company. In 1976, a "New York Times" profile featured Donald Trump as an up-and-coming businessman and society figure. "He is tall, lean and blond with dazzling white teeth," the profile read. "He rides around town in a chauffeured silver Cadillac with his initials—DJT—on his plates. He dates slinky fashion models and at only 30 years of age estimates say that he is worth more than 200 MILLION." Later evidence suggested that he wasn't actually worth that much and maybe his wealth was overstated. But it was also no secret that Trump stood to inherit a lot more millions from his father. He was an up-and-coming king.

> *"Be royal in your own fashion.*
> *Act like a king to be treated like one"*
> — *Robert Greene*

Protecting the Country

Although the Democrats were outraged, Comey had defenders who believed that those encouraging outrage were missing what was more at stake for the nation. When it came to Comey, Daniel Richman, a former federal prosecutor and Comey advisor spoke in his favor. "There are very few people focused on running a government down the road. And I think he is one of them." He also pointed out that, "The desire to have absolute credibility with Congress is absolutely paramount to him." It is also the possibility of reprisal if Congress had learned Comey had information about the Clinton investigation and neglected to inform them. Although it appeared to be bad for Comey, it is possible that things could have gotten worse. If it had leaked out after the election that he'd withheld information, that would have been political suicide and total credibility damage. The election would have been in doubt and probably for the next four years, the next President would be embroiled in more criminal investigations.

The political testing of justice in America may have only just begun, according to "The World" and "Time" magazines. And according to Sam Frizell, "In a span of months, national divisions have torn the very fabric of the institutions on which the nation's identity is based: the credibility of a free press; the integrity of a free election process; the ability of political leaders to carry on a debate of ideas. Comey can be counted as one who saw the dangers coming and did what he could to protect the founding principles of the country. Like so many others, he appears for the moment to have failed."

"It is obvious there was an intent to protect, but from what or from who?"
— Mr. Patterson

WE PUBLISH THE REALIST BOOKS

Chapter Twenty

Election Influenced

Comey tried to control political and corporate scandal which can hit snags in criminal justice. His solution for an uncustomary situation was "uncustomary." Where secrecy functions to protect those who are innocent and warrant fairness, Comey assured Congress that he would keep them informed about any future changes or turn of events in the Clinton investigation which is why he felt compelled to alert Congress about the newly discovered emails found on the computer of the husband of Hillary's closest aide. The husband was under a totally different investigation for allegedly sexting with a minor.

The federal government officials unmasked the Bureau and found that they held off on taking noticeable steps in two other highly politically sensitive investigations. They were prepared to pursue possible criminal activities oversees by Trump's former campaign manager and the Clinton Foundation was another. But Comey felt he was only being noble when he alerted Congress and opened a floodgate of rumors, leaks and prejudice. It was also revealed that Comey had publicly defied telling the world that Russia, with Vladimir Putin's permission, was accountable for the hack of Hillary Clinton's campaign emails. "It could influence the election," he argued. "You either prosecute and proceed or you shut up!" said Don Ayers, a former Deputy Attorney General under George H.W. Bush. "Comey put himself into a box he never should have put himself in."

When Comey publicly testified about the Clinton case, he committed a terrible sin. Democrats came together to express their disappointment by denouncing the prospect of Comey swinging an election with potentially no hard evidence. "They're going to teach this case in law school as what not to do," Michael Chertoff said, Secretary of Homeland Security under former President George W. Bush. Former House Speaker Newt Gingrich, Iowa Senator Chuck Grassley and Ohio Representative Jim Jordan all joined in on the criticism. "I support calls for the FBI to release as much as it can before the election so the voters can make an informed decision," Jim Jordan told "Time" magazine. It was rumored that the Justice Department would possibly do just that. They actually indicated there could be another surprise in the final week of the campaign.

Now, it was beginning to appear that the Justice Department was participating in the way America was voting which was totally crossing the line. The bottom line was that the nation's most powerful law enforcement agency had become the target of unyielding reproach by the same people who at one time were overly excited about Comey's appointment to lead the FBI. It was evident when nearly 100 former Justice Department officials portrayed the decision by the Director to alert Congress of the newly found emails as nothing short of "astonishing" that close to the election. That was not good for the Director because people were beginning to question his motive. "We cannot recall a prior instance where a senior Justice Department official—Republican or Democrat—has, on the eve of a major election, issued a public statement where the mere disclosure of information might impact the election's outcome," former officials, including former Attorney General Eric Holder wrote.

Comey's decision threatened to hurtle a dark cloud on the rest of his remaining years as the Director. It has been a long-standing policy of the Justice Department to never take action in advance of an election that could likely interfere with the outcome. "I have great personal respect for Director Comey and I sincerely believe that he is a man of integrity, independence and good intentions, but I have grave concerns that the credibility of the FBI could be damaged in immeasurable ways," said Representative Elijah Cummings, ranking Democrat on the House Oversight and Government Reform Committee. It was surprising to hear those words when Cummings was one of Comey's most vocal advocates. He also believed the FBI's institutional integrity was hanging in the balance because of Comey's decision. But he once told the Director, based on his first decision not to recommend criminal charges against Hillary Clinton and others involved in the mishandling of classified information. "I don't know whether your family is watching this," Cummings said, "but I hope that they are as proud of you as I am."

But Cummings and 100 other officials quickly changed their opinions about the Director.

"Nobody is above the law"
— *Barack Obama*

Hillary Rodham Clinton

Why Hillary

Donald J. Trump makes history for being the first President to be considered not endorsable and a major party candidate considered to be the least fit for the presidency, ever. "Hillary Clinton is the only choice to keep America great," said Joe Klein. "I've never actually endorsed a candidate. It's not my job. Endorsements are official. They are the prerogative of ownership. But I want to be clear that in this crucial year [2016] I will be voting for Hillary Clinton on November 8th. Not happily," he expressed, "even though I've known her for a long time; known her to be hardworking, intelligent, moral and sane. Not happily," he reiterated. "I sense that she has been too severely damaged in the course of her 30-year battering she's received at the hands of extremists and the media. She may be too defensive now to be courageous in office. Her reignited email scandal reminds us that the Clinton's come fully equipped with a menagerie; a clown show of paranoid retainers, some who should never be allowed anywhere near the Oval Office."

Klein goes on to say, "Clinton is a reminder, too, of the reflexive entitlement that comes with dynastic politics. The Democrats, in general, seem stale.   They represent a boundless faith in government that doesn't acknowledge the corroded inefficiencies of our current system. They practice a form of identity politics—special treatment for special groups—that can easily be perverted; a vulnerability Trump has been exploiting all year. After all, how far is Trump's sense of systemic ethnic depredation—Mexicans as rapists, Muslims as terrorists—from Clinton's view of systemic prejudice with blacks, Latinos and women as the victims? They exist on the same spectrum: group identity as more definitive than individual character. Trump's use of these words which are implicitly vile are 'the blacks,' 'Hispanics,' 'the Muslims,' 'the women,' and yes even 'the veterans.' His stereotypes deny the fabulous array of opportunities that America affords. I'm not sure how real his pessimism—or much else about him—is. But it is ugly and dark in a way this country shouldn't be."

Decent people, including former President Barack Obama agrees with Joe Klein who said, "There is one part of Trump that is indisputably real: his ego. He is personal freedom off the rails, a peculiar American disease. When I think of Trump as a businessman I also think of my father who is a businessman and would sooner forgo a family vacation than stiff a contractor as Trump did. When I think of a celebrity I think of my daughter forcing me to watch an episode of 'Jersey Shore' some years ago because you just couldn't imagine how awful they were. Trump doesn't live in the same universe as Harry Truman. He belongs to the same universe as Snookie. And his supporters know it. They take vengeful pleasure in his profound lack of seriousness. They protest anything complex. Why can't we take Mosul in three days? Why can't we have manufacturing jobs and cheap goods at Wal-Mart at the same time? Why can't we just have immigrants from Europe?

Trump is all about what has gone wrong in our society and nothing about what has gone well. He is about putting his name on buildings he doesn't own; about not paying his taxes; about a charitable foundation that spends its money on self-aggrandizement; and about beauty pageants where he can invade dressing rooms and ogle nude teenagers. He has even debased the notion of luxury with his gilt parody of the good life. He does not read. He doesn't have the patience to be briefed or, worse, to discern between reality and crazy conspiracy theories nor between propaganda and truth. His acceptance of Russia's attacks on our electoral system is unprecedented and outrageous. He upends stability because he doesn't know enough to value it. Those who would put Hilary's failings in the same league as Trump's depravities are delusional.

From the start, people have said to me, 'Well, okay, Trump is about as honest as his hair but he's touching a very real nerve out there.' True, but he is the avatar of easy answers; a leader for those fearful of the unfamiliar. He embodies the notion that engaged citizenship is just too hard for average folks. That compromise is just too complex. He runs, weirdly, against the art of the deal. And he is all ours. He could only happen here."

"Only in America," as Don King would say.
— Joe Klein

"Never stop believing that fighting for what's right is worth it."
— Hillary Clinton

Many women had one goal in their minds and hearts and that was "to crack the country's highest glass ceiling." But doubt was bred as election night got later and later. The key swing states the expected Madam President believed she had in the bag would come with a reality check. Women hit the polls expecting to say the two words they had waited to hear their entire lives—"Madam President." Women and men wore white as a nod to the suffrage movement that finally granted women the right to vote in 1920. Women from all over visited the grave of Susan B. Anthony, the women' rights crusader, who famously cast a ballot in 1872 although she knew it was illegal. For her valiant act she was arrested. A voter who was born before she got the right to vote stated, "I'd like to vote twice but that's not possible." She was 100 years old and her name was Florence Thaler from Pequannock Township, New Jersey.

Women walked up to the polls with their daughters, sisters, mothers and grandmothers. It was a day for the women and they were excited. "This is a weird day," Tweeted Lucy Arnold. Elizabeth Wilson played Beyoncé's song "Run the World Girls" and Fleetwood Mac's "Don't Stop" on her Instagram, documenting the morning walk to her polling station. "I was feeling excited, ecstatic, happy and lucky to be a part of this historic moment," Wilson said. "The country's been ready for a few decades for a woman President." But by Tuesday night things began to look gloomy. The voting margins were very close with Clinton eventually losing. "I never cried when I've filled out my ballot before but then I realized my daughters—and I have three of them—have a right to vote for a woman. It made me cry."

But she would cry again when the night ended. Hillary was possibly the best choice if one was judging principles and morals, and if it was the desire of the voter to finally see a woman become President of the United States. "I thought it was great that a black man got elected for President," 103-year old Ruline Steininger said. "I didn't think that would happen in my lifetime, but it did. Now, it is high time for a woman and this time we have a woman who is really capable of being President of the United States." Even the estranged wife of Donald J. Trump thought Hillary Clinton would be the first woman President although, secretly, she was wrong.

"Millions of women had one goal in mind: To crack the country's highest glass ceiling once and for all."
— *"USA Today"*

But in 2016, it would not happen.

American   Money   Publishing

WE PUBLISH THE REALIST BOOKS

Chapter Twenty-one

The American Dream

It has been planted into the black's psyche that Democrats are for them and they "got their backs." But in reality:

> *"The Democrats have created*
> *the biggest trickery against*
> *blacks since their own people captured them and*
> *sold them to the white people for slavery."*
> — *Patterson*

America has allowed foreign immigrants to enter the United States with benefits; giving them the opportunity to go to school, receive a good education and provide them with loans to help them start a business. But blacks were kidnapped and forced to come to this country. Once they became citizens, they were not afforded any special benefits to assist them in rising above their struggles. It's as if the U.S. don't want to see the black man rise. Democrats offered them "welfare" which is designed to keep black people broke. White's don't want or accept welfare and if they do they're considered "white trash." Immigrants will receive visas and loans to pay for their education. However, for a black to receive a scholarship they must be exceptional in sports. We know the white's feel it was their country first and they should benefit first, but blacks helped build this country without pay and so they should come in a close second.

But instead, people from foreign countries get treated better than blacks. Democrats didn't do blacks any favors by offering welfare. That was a trick. Then Democrats tricked blacks again with new laws designed to keep them in prison for a minimum 10 years to life. There are blacks doing a lifetime in prison for non-violent crimes—all because of Bill and Hillary Clinton. That was the biggest trick in history. It put blacks in prison to become slaves again but this time it's at 8 cents an hour, and they take 55% of that. This is very profitable for the country but devastating for blacks. Blacks have fought in every war America has participated in but still have been left out when it comes to benefits for its citizens. Most immigrants have never fought for America and are taking food and money from African-Americans. During the Martin Luther King marches to reverse Jim Crow laws, few immigrants were marching for the rights of Americans. Bill and Hillary put so many blacks in prison that they depopulated the black race, destroying families as they imprisoned husbands and fathers. This trick was also done on the federal level. If a black person had five grams of crack-cocaine he would get a 10-year minimum sentence whereas a white could get caught with three kilograms and get three years. They called it a "war on drugs" but it was a war on blacks. If an immigrant has crossed the border illegally into the U.S. and they have children in the U.S., their children should not be considered a legal citizen. How can they when their existence started with an illegal act?

Blacks receive the harshest punishments for crimes committed by blacks. Blacks were forced into lives of crime because they were denied good jobs. Therefore, they sold small amounts of drugs or became pimps. Although those crimes are bad, they're not violent crimes. Child molesters, who are usually white, will receive a lesser sentence than a black who did not commit a violent crime. The black politicians are no better. They lie to blacks to line their pockets. They're like the new "house nigger" who worked in the slave master's house and not in the field. Blacks don't know their history therefore they don't know their real surnames. Most of them still carry the last name of their grandfather's slave master. Blacks and eventually immigrants were brought to America to help build it but at the end of the day, the blacks are left with nothing; nothing to work for and nothing to show for. How is that the American dream?

"It's more like the American nightmare,
but only for blacks."
— *Patterson*

Blacks are American not immigrants. Therefore, they should inherit the fruit of the land. Blacks did not migrate to America. They were brought here.

IN 1619 THE HOUSE OF BURGESSES FIRST REPESENTATIVE ASSEMBLY IN THE NEW WORLD, ELECTED JULY 30 AT JAMESTOWN, VIRGINIA FIRST BLACK LABORERS—INDENTURED SERVANTS—IN ENGLISH NORTH AMERICAN COLONIES, BROUGHT

BY THE DUTCH TO JAMESTOWN IN AUGUST. CHATTEL SLAVERY LEGALLY RECOGNIZED. 1650

Therefore, when blacks were brought to America they were considered transferable property which made blacks legal citizens, and clearly makes blacks American citizens.

Take the Country Back

It took 160 years for the Republicans to abolish slavery and provide the votes to Congress to pass the Civil Rights Bill which helped bring the Cold War to a close. Now the country was in fear that Trump could ruin all the progress. He said he would kill the families of terrorists, has crazy conspiracy theories and is adamant about building a wall. The outcome for America could be disastrous when Trump is done. He hasn't even begun to make his first move but if stopped today, he has already done real damage. His beliefs are abnormal; they lack substance and are out of tune with reality. They are filled with conflict with no regard for facts. It is noted that when he was younger Trump spent a summer on one of his father's construction sites in New York. "I worked alongside carpenters, plumbers and men carrying heavy scaffolding poles." He claims that was the experience that showed him he needed to be concerned about hardworking, blue collar men who he believed had been left behind by American politics. This is why today he feels so deeply rooted in economic nationalism.

For decades he has railed against trade deals. He had a standoff with NAFTA (North American Free Trade Agreement) in the early 90's. He said, "It's the worst trade deal in history." In his view he makes no secret that America's trade deficit is proof of foul play or very bad negotiating skills. He preaches that more trade deals would be cataclysmic and American companies need to move back to the United States. He holds deep underlying instincts but he might be willing to bargain over the penalties they should pay. Trump is a protectionist who eventually got 65 million people to agree with him. America's enemies were rooting for Trump to be the next President. They harped on his geographical and diplomatic ignorance. But Trump is a master at business and therefore wants all those places outside of America to pay the full cost of America's dominating protection. Trump argues that allies should have to show more appreciation for

American bases to be on their soil as well as for the expense of equipping and paying the soldiers.

We can't just call it isolationism because Trump acquired some foreign ventures which included the work of Iraq and seizure of its oilfields. He envisions like a Roman of foreign policy. He feels the rest of the world must pay tribute to the capitol and be grateful for the military troops. "I appreciate any candidate that's gonna keep jobs in America," a Trump supporter said. Trump promises big plans for infrastructure spending and putting millions of people to work while he rebuilds it. He was the only candidate who spoke on the mass layoff of workers which got a lot of blue-collar worker's attentions. "Finally, somebody gives a damn that my dad lost his job," a supporter said. Trump stood in front of a huge crowd and told the world, "We have to take our country back!" The Trump triumph has the world on edge and could be a tragedy for the Republicans, for the country and for the rest of the world. As President of the United States, Trump is more powerful than any man on earth. Plus, he is filthy rich. At this moment in time he is unstoppable.

"Work on the hearts and minds of others."
— *Robert Greene*

Chapter Twenty-two

Unusual Tactics

As Trump launched into the real estate game he broke with his millionaire father who had warned him against taking on too much debt. He told him it wasn't smart to try and take on the tough market of Manhattan, but Donald had a hunger to go to the next level and build in Midtown. He also wanted his building to be bigger and brasher than any other building. He became a leader in his field big-time with tough, loud and showy tactics he would continue to use for decades. He is the mastermind behind creating his own image of himself. He projected himself as a rich playboy with the best connections. He used his image to actually make the best deals with other rich and powerful men. He made his competitors, regulators and even bankers believe he was more powerful and rich than what he really was. He out-smarted and manipulated every person he needed to accomplish his goals. He had a knack for neutralizing or even winning over his opponents by attacking, threatening or sometimes hiring them so they could be on his side.

On his very first project—during the rehab of New York's disastrous Commodore Hotel—Trump had a problem he needed solved but they refused to oblige him. He was nobody and he realized he needed to make them think he was somebody. That's when he persuaded a "New York Times" reporter to write an article about him as if he was a major New York builder; he had yet to build one building. But Trump was smart and realize early in the game he had to take shortcuts. When he needed top New York politicians' cooperation to get his hotel project underway, he made the decision to hire Governor Hugh Carey's chief fundraiser who obviously had key political connections. And as an added bonus, he chose the Governor that his father had donated more money to his campaign than anyone other than the candidate's brother.

During the same project he needed a tax exemption from a state authority created so he could build racially integrated housing. City politicians opposed the tax incentive and called a news conference outside the shuttered hotel. That's when Trump threatened to abandon the project. He also took off the cover and replaced the clean boards that covered the once grand hotel's windows with dirty scrap wood, making the building a "sore eye" for the city. That was the "nail in the coffin" and Trump got his exemption. And for decade after decade Trump led his empire through many defeats, triumphs and disasters; through conquest of the Atlantic City Casino world and through six corporate bankruptcies while still making the media believe that he was having no problems.

"The key way I promote is bravado. I play to peoples fantasies. People may not think big themselves, but they can still get very excited by those who do."
— *Donald J. Trump*

In his book *The Art of the Deal* he wrote,

"From a pure business point of view, the benefits of being

written about have far outweighed the drawbacks...even a critical story which may be hurtful personally can be very valuable to your business."
— *Donald J. Trump*

It didn't matter if Trump lied and people wrote about it. He would continue to tell the lie, newspapers and magazines would continue to write about it and people would begin to believe it was the truth. The big lie would eventually become the truth if you repeated it enough.

"My best value is motivating workers and winning media attention."
— *Donald J. Trump*

He has always calculated his success by the reach and power of his reputation and image. All of his business ventures were based on the Trump name which represented success, wealth and ambition. His businesses included gambling, TV, politics and sports which were all designed to spotlight the name Trump.

Shaking in Their Boots

"They are the men who,
with their flesh and blood, buy victory.
You can smash from the air,
pound to rubble with artillery,
thrust though with armor,
but always these men on foot, the
men with rifles and bayonets
and steady sloggin' courage,
must go on. Without them all else is in vain."
— *R.W. Thompson,*
March 1, 1945

"On Veterans Day we must pause to reflect on the courage, dedication and loyalty of our nation's military veterans. Throughout history their hard work and sacrifice have kept us safe and protected our freedom. We owe them a debt of gratitude that can never be repaid so we salute them for their service. To all of the brave men and women who have sacrificed to put our country first, we thank you and America thanks you. Everyone should salute and respect you." But Trump showed no respect for Senator John McCain when he stated,

"I don't like soldiers who get caught. I like winners who get away." John McCain had been a soldier of war who was captured but fortunately, after many years and hardships, he was rescued and made it back to the United States; but only when all his men were able to return to the U.S. He would not go and leave them there.

John McCain, the Senator of Arizona said, "The blustery billionaire has gone too far!" Trump fired back with, "Prisoners of war make poor heroes." This meant every soldier of war who was captured during wars the U.S. participated in could never be a hero in Trump's eyes. How can a man, the elected leader of the United States, have so little regard for the men and women who fought for America to be great? How can he show little support for our prisoners of war and then want to say, "Let's make America great again?" He's a hypocrite! He's contradicting himself, especially as he's never been a soldier of war. He sits in his comfortable chair behind his huge desk and gives orders. He's never been dirty, tired, hurt or wounded on a battlefield but he has passed judgment on those who have sacrificed their lives; those who have lost arms, legs, sight and in the ultimate case, their lives.

Trump's economic plan which includes the military is fantastical. He has promised to diminish America's nine trillion dollar national debt while he is President and at the same time implement the biggest tax cut—ten trillion dollars—in decades. He has also vowed to protect Social Security. The Committee for a Responsible Federal Budget, an Apostle Group, has pointed out that he would not be able to accomplish his goal without having to cut other areas of government by at least 93%. But Trump adamantly disagrees. "I will improve America's trade terms from the factory killing Chinese trade negotiators." He has accused China of "raping America." He explained that the savings from the improvement of the agreements would render the government more fruitful. He was challenged with won't contributions to government waste and abuse make America's four trillion federal budget miniscule? "No, all over government," Trump roared back. "And I'll tell you where there's tremendous, tremendous money being spent: it's on the military. And yet I'm going to build it up for us, not every country in the world. We're spending massive amounts of money to protect other nations."

With this type of outcry it is no doubt other countries should be shaking in their boots and thinking that with Trump as the new President, the United States will possibly abandon assisting less powerful countries. Not only has he abandoned the respect Americans have for veterans and war heroes, he has plans to not assist in fighting wars with our allies or vulnerable countries. He plans to ditch America's trade agreements in favor of short-term bilateral negotiations undertaken in a spirit so vicious it would surely make trade wars with China inevitable. Trump said he is not afraid of the outcome, whether with a rival property developer or the world's second biggest economy. "They can't afford it, we can," Trump boasted. "We have a trade deficit with China of hundreds of billions of dollars a year." Which wouldn't be smart to buck.

"When you're powerful, you fear nothing and no one."

— Mr. Genaro

Chapter Twenty-three

Either Choice, Bad...

The Presidential Election of 2016 was unlike any in modern U.S. history and likely the history of the United States. Both candidates who promised to lead the nation were widely unpopular, couldn't be trusted and were possibly racist. Neither appeared particularly prepared to handle such a role that would convince Americans they could bring America together; and neither could present a compelling vision. According to a definition of leadership outlined at Mindtools.com, "Leaders help themselves and others do the right thing. They set direction, build an inspiring vision and create something new. Leadership is about mapping out where you need to go to 'win' as a team or an organization and it is dynamic, exiting and inspiring. Yet, while leaders set the direction, they must also use management skills to guide their people to the right destination in a smooth and efficient way." This definition lacks a description for either candidate—Hillary Clinton or Donald Trump.

Neither outlined an effective vision for the country. Maybe they possibly could if public contempt and mistrust did not exist because both of them spoke truthful messages that needed to be heard. But while Hillary tried to convince voters that America was already and had always been great, her nemesis vowed to make America great again which meant America was not so great again. Hillary continued to pretend that the country was not a deeply troubled nation while Trump pandered to "white victim syndrome" by pointing out all the things which plagued whites. But America cannot be great. It has committed too many sins against the Bible and God himself. She has failed and thus will suffer Godlike castigation for the cruel and unusual mistreatment of black women, children and men she once enslaved. Blacks believe the American dream is an illusion and soon Mexicans will feel the same. According to "The Final Call," "We cannot have faith in a country where we are slaughtered in the streets and denied justice. We cannot have faith in a nation that has never treated blacks properly. America has to recognize the painful truth and make an agonizing decision for a people who have always clung to their slave masters and former slave masters. If America's leaders cannot save their nation, how can they save blacks?" The best thing about the election was that it acquainted blacks with the reality of a falling and fading empire which has ruled for centuries. But if America doesn't change, it will have a crushing ending.

Raping America

Trump believes that America is in serious trouble. He inflates and conflates these troubles into an absurd caricature of failure and decline. "We are like a third world country. America makes the worst trade deals ever in the history of the trade...We've spent four million dollars in the Middle East and we're in far worse shape than we were before...China, it doesn't respect us." Trump believes that China is raping America and the Mexicans are raping American women. He blames this on "crooked," incompetent politicians. He targets the most exaggeratedly, down-in-the-mouth Americans who indulge in their meanest instincts;

the ones who feel what they feel; the ones who want vengeance, ready respond with violence which on occasions have exacted real harm.

With his pick of Senator Sessions, who was rejected as a federal judge because of his racial remarks, Trump will enhance America's mass incarceration problem. He called the NAACP un-American and he is totally in favor of deporting immigrants back and keeping immigrants out of the United States. Bannon says, "Darkness is good." He was formerly appointed a high position in Trump's Administration. "Trump is scary," says Jim Adkins, the manager of an Olive Garden restaurant. He voted for Hillary Clinton although he was a Republican. But this time he overcame his dislike for Mrs. Clinton. Another election volunteer said, "Many Republican voters are defecting to the other side" thanks to the seemingly unstoppable rise of Donald Trump. Like Hitler, he abhors there being a different race than "white." Like Hitler, he surrounds himself with people who are white supremacists. And like Hitler, he appears to be a fascist. His appointments are controversial hard-liners who are bigots and racists. It looks as if Donald Trump will be the one who rapes America. He will forever be remembered for his hate and his racism and no longer for his Trump hotels and the Trump name. (In 1866, Congress took control of Southern Reconstruction, backed Freedmen's rights in legislation which was vetoed by Johnson; Veto was overridden by Congress April 9th, Ku Klux Klan secretly formed in the South to terrorize blacks who voted. Disbanded 1869 - 1871).

AMP

American   Money   Publishing

WE PUBLISH THE REALIST BOOKS

Chapter Twenty-four

The Trump Empire

Trump's first project was also considered extreme. It was not only big for the break-out developer but it was big for Manhattan, New York. It was the Grand Hyatt Hotel which he built near the Grand Central railroad terminal. This project was a 58-story Manhattan skyscraper and the tower eventually became Trump's primary residence and headquarters of the Trump Organization. But that was only the beginning for the real estate mogul. After the Manhattan Grand Hyatt Hotel and the Trump Tower he continued to build. His empire included the Plaza Hotel and a share of the Empire State Building.

Trump became a master at real estate development and continued to build other buildings including the 92-story Trump International Hotel and Tower Chicago in Chicago, Illinois. He also purchased the historic Mar-a-Lago estate in Palm Beach, Florida. Then he upgraded and expanded the mansion that was built in the 1920's and converted it into an exclusive "members only" club. He had become one of the hardest working men in real estate development. He was sought out by other developers for his expertise and know-how. He had a gift for making the best deals and could build projects under cost and deliver them ahead of schedule. He also developed a number of Casinos and hotels in Atlantic City, New Jersey, although they had some drawbacks which created situations where he had to file for bankruptcy. But Trump was brilliant and established the company in a way where he was able to protect all his personal assets from the risk of corporate bankruptcy.

The Trump Empire also added a number of golf courses including those in Dubai, Scotland, Ireland and across the United States. The Trump Organization added a wide selection of Trump-brand products. Over the years he has added menswear, steaks, neckties, mattresses, spring water and cologne. Trump also founded Trump University, a for-profit real estate training program. But it was one of his businesses not profitable for him and in 2010, when a lawsuit accused its managers of illegal business practices, went under and is now defunct. Trump imitated his father in many ways, including contributing money to politicians who he believed could sway decisions that would be in favor of his business practices. He made contributions to Democrats and Republicans. He even donated money to Hillary Rodham Clinton for her campaigns for senator and for her race to the White House in 2008. It was ironic that in 2016 Trump would run against her and win. Trump has always been a winner, even when he loses. What's on everyone's mind is, "How Trump won?"

TRUMP WINS...
HE BECOMES THE NEW
PRESIDENT-ELECT...

Mandate

Trump believes his presidency is a mandate, not realizing that a man can have it all and still have nothing. While Trump stands at his window in Trump Towers, he looks down on the little people of the world. "I have the whole world in my hands," he whispers to himself. He vows to make America great again but because of his vision and newfound power, evil is running rampant through the streets. The world is beginning to believe that Trump is the core of that evil. Wise men whisper amongst each other, trying to think of a way to stop him before it's too late. "As long as there is evil, good will rise up to defeat it," one wise man said. "Well, someone needs to rise soon," responded one of the others. Destiny is not the path given but it is the path a man must choose to reach it. Trump has created a path to his destiny that is very enriching and powerful. It's a path he would like his children to follow.

Trump is seeking out other rich people to be a part of his Administration as well as considering people who are not favorable in the eyes of America's top allies. When he considered Mitt Romney top allies spoke against him, issuing warnings against appointing him. Plus, during the campaign, they were both at each other's throat. But maybe Donald wanted to keep his enemy close. Donald Trump may sometimes appear stupid, but he is not; not by a long shot. Some would say he is extremely smart and there is a method to everything he does. Another stated Trump is a big man; big enough to look past the debate issues he had with Mitt Romney. He knew Romney had some foreign intelligence and could be useful. "Russia is the greatest strategic threat," Romney once said, and it's likely he is correct. Trump also knew that with Romney he could unify the party. He sometimes made decisions to restore their bond and trust but would turn around and make another decision that would completely contradict the first, again, keeping everyone around him and the world off-balance.

Trump told the world, "We need to take back our country," and he meant every word of it. He mastered the skill of getting people to vote who had never voted before. Trump also met with Nigel Farage, interim leader of the UK Independence Party (UKIP) and member of the European Parliament. Trump met with him days after being elected which was not a great message to send to the British Prime Minister. He also chose Michael Flynn who blatantly called Islam a cancer. He met with James "Mad Dog" Mattis, the real deal, as his possible choice for Secretary of Defense. Although Trump was not yet in the White House, he held those high-profile meetings up in Trump Towers. He believes his presidency is a mandate but other men of power have reportedly said it is not.

Trump can't just give an order which will cause men to be killed as a dictator would. He can't just change laws without them being voted on. Well, actually he can. And what gives him the power to do all those things is the Republican Party because they are the majority in Congress and will back Donald Trump. Nigel Farage said, "I backed Trump because I thought the man had guts and integrity and boy he has! "I found the President-elect has the makings to be a great President."

Nigel Farage

But at the same time Trump's son-in-law, Jerry Kushner, was rubbing United States' allies the wrong way. However, that didn't stop Giuliani from staying right behind Trump and defending him all the way. "I think he's going to put together an extraordinary Administration. He has a lot of good people around him." But the rest of the world didn't see it that way. It appeared as if he was choosing persons who would pass all the new laws he wanted to implement which would give him the power of a dictator.

The nation's biggest complaint was Trump's choice of Stephen Bannon, the former head of "Breitbart News Network." He pushed for a darker and more divisive populism; publishing articles which stirred racial animus. Trump appointed him as White House Chief Strategist. He also tapped Reince Priebus, the Republican Party Chairman, as Chief of Staff. "I am trained to have my very successful team continue with me in leading the country," Trump said. "Now I will have Steve and Reince with me in the White House as we work to make America great again." But the world did not feel as confident.

Stephen Bannon

THE RABBLE-ROUSER. The former head of "Breitbart," Stephen Bannon has pushed for a darker and more divisive populism, publishing articles that stirred racial animus.

Chapter Twenty-five

The Red Meat

Once Trump became the President-elect, he wasted no time in picking the members of his Cabinet to be a part of his White House white world circle. It became obvious that he would surround himself with a cast of neocons, white nationalists and military officials who had been accused of war crimes. He began appointing white supremacists in high positions. "So far, the transition is still feeding what is now the Republican Party, the "RED MEAT'! The appointment of some of these guys, especially Steve Bannon, was a clear signal that he was going to have white supremacists at the highest levels of government," said Dr. Ray Winbush, Director of the Institute for Urban Research at Morgan State University.

Trump also picked Alabama Senator Jeff Sessions, as the new Attorney General. Sessions, a former prosecutor, became a senator in 1996. He has always supported anti-immigration legislation. He was also a leading proponent of efforts to repeal the 14th Amendment which guarantees citizenship to every child born in the United States. And, he was always outspoken on the Voting Rights Act. He was nominated as a federal judge by President Reagan in 1986, but he was denied confirmation because of his racist comments from his past. He stated that he thought the Ku Klux Klan was okay until he found out they smoked marijuana.

Trump offered Lieutenant General Michael Flynn the position of National Security Advisor. He expressed during his campaign that he wanted to stop immigrants from entering the U.S. which is why he most likely selected Jeff Sessions. He also said he didn't want Muslims in the United States and General Flynn is well-known for his anti-Muslim worldview, having called Islam a cancer and said, "Fear of Muslims is rational." If Trump wanted Flynn, he would be in because the position of National Security Advisor does not require Senate confirmation. Flynn served as the Director of the Defense Intelligence Agency under President Obama where his subordinates referred to him as "Flynn Facts" in response to false claims he often made; claiming Sharia Law was spreading throughout the U.S.

Michael (Mike) Pence

THE VICE PRESIDENT OF THE UNITED STATES

Another pick by Trump was Republican Kansas Congressman Mike Pompeo. He was once a CIA Director and opposed closing Guantanamo Bay

Prison which was the same way Trump felt. In 2013, Pompeo made a visit to the disreputable prison to get a first-hand look at the prisoners who were on a hunger strike. "It looked to me like a lot of them had put on weight." He was also very outspoken on the six-nation Iran nuclear deal.

Dr. Winbush believed that in reality it would be Mike Pence who would be running the White House because he doesn't believe Donald Trump knows what he is doing. "He's really going to be calling the shots," Winbush said. "Black people have got to get serious about organizing just as white supremacists are strengthening. They see Trump's victory as a victory for them." Winbush also said, "We celebrated Obama's victory and—and this is not a criticism of Obama—but Obama did not appoint key people to his Administration that were directly related to the people who put him in office, namely black people. Trump is actually doing that. He is beholden to the white supremacists; the KKK and the alt-right. He is literally appealing to the base that put him in office."

"Without loyalty, you have nothing."

— *Mr. Genaro*

Trump has always worked with a tiny inner circle top executives—his campaign staff was about a 10th the size of Hillary Clinton's—and remained loyal to those who play by his rules. No one would step out on their own, all credit goes to the boss and the message to the public was that Trump, the man, was the rainmaker and not the corporation or its executives. He believes in loyalty to his people and if he feels betrayed, he will do everything possible to destroy them.

"You have to realize that people—sadly, sadly—are very vicious."
— Donald J. Trump

He surrounds himself with smart people who are loyal. He expects them to look the part, something he has always expressed throughout the years. But how he makes his decisions to choose people is usually subtle. He is accustomed to hiring people who have been obstacles to his projects. He would do that to neutralize his opposition and to utilize their knowledge. He would also hire to create rival power centers just as he had done with his Cabinet picks. Most GOP leaders believed or thought Trump would be forced to choose between

Republican National Committee Chairman Reince Priebus and former "Breitbart News Network" Chairman Stephen Bannon to set the tone for the leadership of his White House. "But Trump hired both men, the establishment choice and the rogue outsider, and gave them equal billing in his hiring announcement."

Donald Trump and Mike Pence

American　　　Money　　　Publishing

WE PUBLISH THE REALIST BOOKS

Chapter Twenty-six

Against Gun Rights

"If Clinton opposes American's right to bear arms, she should just come out and say so instead of blatantly lying."

— Donald Trump

During the last Presidential debate there was a lot of talk about gun control and the 2nd Amendment. Hillary Clinton was asked her stance on the 2nd Amendment and David French believed she answered dishonestly. "Her response was so dishonest I literally laughed at the television screen." Hillary went back and forth on the issue and was sometimes confusing. She would say she believed in a person's right to bear arms then turn around and admit she did not agree with the *District of*

Columbia vs. Heller ruling which set precedence from the Supreme Court in 2008. It was a landmark case that struck down a cruel gun control law that forbids D.C. residences from owning handguns; shotguns and/or rifles had to be kept unloaded and disassembled or secured by trigger lock.

The Supreme Court ruled the law was a violation of the Constitution. It violated the 2nd Amendment right of citizens to own guns for self-defense. But Hillary attempted to defend her stand on the law by telling the world on national TV that she disagreed with the ruling only because she wanted to protect toddlers from guns. But her non-supporters did not accept that excuse. They believed the landmark ruling of "Heller" had nothing to do with protecting children. The "Wall Street Journal" said, "If she is elected, say goodbye to the right to bear arms," which is possibly another reason why voters chose not to elect Hillary Clinton as the next President. The people knew that if Hillary won she would appoint a liberal and the "Heller" law would be overturned. The Supreme Court would have gotten that fifth vote and that was something the people did not want. On the other hand, Donald Trump made it clear that with him as President, no one would lose their right to bear arms. "That's why this election is so important," said Curt Levy in FoxNews.com. "Today, it's the courts rather than our elected officials who have the final say on the nation's most bitterly contested legal and political disputes."

The voters also didn't like the impact Hillary would have on abortion issues if she was elected the next President. In the final Presidential debate she stated, "I will defend *Roe vs. Wade* and I will defend women's rights to make their own healthcare decisions." And after Donald Trump attacked her on late term abortions, accusing her of killing living babies, she was labeled "Killary Clinton" which made a lot of voters look at her as if she was an actual killer, not allowing children to live life.

The Impossible – Possible; Made it Look Easy

All of his life, no matter what he's done; Trump has made it look easy. He made things appear natural and accomplished with ease. He's never used his hands to perform hard labor, although he has built some of the tallest buildings, he's never gotten his hands dirty. He's never gotten his clothing dirty. He's never gotten callouses on his hands. He's executed countless business and real estate deals which made him seem the smartest man in real estate. He made 100 million dollar deals behind his desk in the Trump Tower and in the leather seats on the Trump plane and helicopter. He believes in the notion that there is no limit to what he can accomplish. All of his ventures look effortless, and even when he does have problems he paints a picture that there is none. He turns problems into new solutions. He will never reveal any mistakes, issues or disasters.

Trump has a gift for making something that is difficult to build look easy. He made a difficult race to win look easy without ever revealing if he had any doubts. It is human nature to admire the achievements of some unusual feat. But if it is accomplished naturally and gracefully, our admiration increases tenfold. "Whereas...to labor at what one is doing and...to make bones over it, shows an extreme lack of grace and causes everything, whatever it's worth, to be discounted." To give the impression that you are not ordinary but instead extraordinary, your power depends specifically on your visual appearance and the illusions you create. His buildings are his artwork; creating masterpieces of visual appeal that have amazed its audience, including everybody who ever visited them, occupied them, or just walked past them. It makes you wonder, "How does he do it?"

But Trump would never reveal all of his secrets. He is a specialist at keeping people in suspense with his unorthodox moves and vocabulary. He knew that if a man reveals his secrets about how to easily accomplish so much so fast, he'll become just one more mortal among other men. When people learn your secrets your accomplishments are no longer awe-inspiring. Some of us can look at his buildings and say to ourselves, "I can do that," if we had his money, a rich father and all his connections. But without knowing his secrets we will still doubt ourselves. Clever men avoid the temptations of showing how smart they are. It is always more clever to conceal your magic and keep those who admire you always wondering, "How does he do it?"

This is what enhances the aura which surrounds Trump. He keeps the world guessing while he appears immortal. He doesn't work hard; he hardly works. He makes everyone else perform the work: labor, research, deliveries, electricity, plumbing, etc. Trump makes the deals, collects the money and make sure everything happens according to plan. He does all of this without it ever being noticed. He never seems to lift a finger or is under strain. This gives him the impression of having immense power because he accomplishes great things with ease.

Trump can be compared to the Great Houdini. The great escape artist, Harry Houdini, once advertised his act as "The Impossible Possible." He was amazing on stage and those who witnessed the great man in action believed that he contradicted commonsense ideas of human capacity. One of his remembered acts was to escape from a pair of manacles professed to be the strongest ever created. They were built with six sets of locks and nine tumblers in each cuff. It was said that it took five years to make them. They were examined by experts who said they had never seen anything so detailed and complex before. "It would be impossible to escape from them," one expert explained.

Houdini said he could escape from them and he would do it in front of a crowd of 4,000 people. They all watched as the cuffs were secured around his wrists. Then Houdini entered a black cabinet positioned on the stage. Minute after minute passed by which made the crowd start to believe that it was possible the Great Houdini could possibly face his first defeat. Then he emerged to face the audience with the cuffs still on. At that point the crowd thought he was about to admit defeat. "Can you please temporarily remove them so I can remove my coat?" But his request was denied in fear that it could be a trick to figure out how the locks worked on the cuffs. "Okay, no problem," he said. Then he lifted his coat over his shoulders and managed to turn it inside out. With his teeth, he removed a penknife from inside his vest pocket and figured out a way to cut the coat from around his arms and removed the coat himself. The crowd clapped and cheered as he made his way back inside the black cabinet. Houdini was letting the crowd know that although he asked for permission, to remove his coat while handcuffed was not a hard task for him.

Houdini was in the cabinet another 20 to 25 minutes, keeping the crowd in suspense, when finally he emerged with hands completely free. He walked out onto the stage, holding the intricate manacles high in the air. To this day, no one has figured out how he did it. It was reported that he never looked worried or concerned. It is believed he could have escaped in record time but it was his intention to draw out the escape as a way to heighten the drama. He wanted his audience to worry, to squirm and to believe he might fail so when he did escape it made him appear to have pulled off the impossible. To complain about the coat was all a part of his act. But when it was all over he made it look easy. Houdini told the crowd, "These manacles are nothing. I could have freed myself a lot sooner and from a lot worse!"

Just like Trump he would continue to perform incredible feat after feat and make them look easy. After the manacle escape he would escape from the chained carcass of an embalmed "sea monster," which was a half octopus half whale-like creature. He was trapped inside a huge envelope that he escaped from without ripping the paper. He escaped from straightjackets while hanging high in the air. He walked through brick walls and jumped from icy bridges with his hands and legs in chains into icy waters. He even trapped himself inside a thick glass case full of water with his hands padlocked. He did all of this while his audience watched in amazement as he would almost die, struggling to set himself free. Houdini could stay underwater without breathing. On many occasions he barely escaped death. It was as if he was superhuman.

Yet, after each survival he would never reveal how he was able to accomplish the impossible. He would leave his audience and critics in awe as they speculated how he did it. His power and reputation were enhanced by his near-death encounters and his struggles to almost lose his life; then fight for his life. His most perplexing trick was convincing an audience that he could make a ten thousand pound elephant disappear. It was impossible but he did it. He made it happen at his shows for 19 weeks and still no one knows how he did it. Until this day it is still a mystery. People have wondered how he accomplished so many tricks. Some say it was occult forces, psychic abilities and even elaborate gadgets which were used secretly to make his escapes seem effortless. Although no one knows exactly how Houdini was able to accomplish so many great feats, there is one clear distinction: it wasn't magic or the occult or gadgets. What is clear is that he made it look easy and never revealed how he did it. He made himself appear bigger than life, just like Donald J. Trump.

What we know about Houdini is that he perfected his art, never leaving anything to chance. He couldn't or it could mean his early death. He studied day and night. He became an expert in how locks worked. He studied centuries old sleight-of-hand tricks. He mastered mechanics and learned how to utilize muscles in his body others would never use. He stayed lissome and flexible and became proficient in the art of breathing. All of those things played vital parts in his ability to prevail in his challenging career. It is said that he even became skilled at controlling the muscles in his throat because of an old Japanese man—whom he met while touring—who taught him an ancient trick: how to swallow a small ball and then bring it back up. He would practice it all day and night until he perfected it. In the beginning he would use a small, peeled potato tied to a string and practice swallowing it and bringing it back up as he learned how to control his throat muscles. Once he felt he had control, he would swallow and bring the potato back up without the string. With this maneuver he could swallow a key or other small devices and bring it back up.

During his escape of the manacles, the experts searched Houdini's body extensively to make sure he didn't have anything on him to help him escape. But they didn't check his throat. No one would ever believe a man could conceal tools in his throat to help him escape. Therefore, theoretically, everyone was wrong about how he made his great escapes. It was not gadgets. It was his ability to control his muscles, to remain flexible and his research all made it possible for him to make his great escapes. Just like Trump, he was able to awe people by his ability to perform great acts and make them look effortless.

The world admires achievements of unusual feats, especially if it is accomplished naturally and gracefully. That will increase the admiration tenfold. Michelangelo refused to let anybody see his work until it was completed. He would do this because to allow anyone to see how he made his work would tarnish the magic of the effect. It is far cleverer to conceal the workings of a man's cleverness. When you reveal the inner workings of your creation, you become just one more mortal among others.

The 30th Law — The 48 Laws of Power
— Robert Greene

Make your accomplishments seem effortless.

Chapter Twenty-Seven

Erasing the Name

The world grew up on Donald Trump. He was a young kid with a big dream. The world needed Trump and it needed his dream, his mind and his buildings. Trump brought luxury, style and comfort to hotels. He made people feel important; like they were somebody, even if they weren't. He built the most prestigious hotels in the world and everybody loved them. The Trump name was a name of respect, so much so that he turned it into a profit. The name is behind big shows like "The Apprentice" and the Miss Universe Pageant as well as world renowned golf courses. He's a billionaire, celebrity and successful real estate mogul and the world loved him. They followed his love life and his family, wanting to take pictures with the great man.

But Trump would change all that. The world would no longer love the Trump name, the hotels or the Trump family. He would turn himself from someone people once loved into someone people now hated. Trump had erased the name and revealed to the world he really was. People are now protesting in front of his hotels with all that hatred energized toward him. The people were blaming Trump for reigniting hate in America and for dividing the country. Jill Stein demanded a recount of the election and she was joined by the Clinton Administration. Americans have turned their backs on Trump. They refuse to accept him as their President. He finds himself in a daily Tweet war trying to fend off the many attacks against him. It would not be a surprise if he was assassinated just like Abe Lincoln or John F. Kennedy because no President in history has been hated as much as Donald J. Trump. He is hated by immigrants, Mexicans, Muslims whites and African-Americans. But he is loved by those who share his vision. But some of them have had a change of mind since Trump started back-pedaling on some of his promises. This caused them to realize that Trump was just telling them what they wanted to hear. His entire purpose in life is to do whatever he can to put himself in power with no in-betweens. And anybody who believes otherwise is delusional.

As the Trump name and brand diminishes, Ivanka Trump—Donald's ex-wife—is watching her most valuable asset crumble right before her eyes. She has worked for years, leveraging her surname (Trump) to create her own fashion business. The Trump name has been very profitable and useful for Ivanka until his Presidential run. Now the name has become tarnished and it appears to be getting worse by the day. Trump's approval rating among women has fallen. And Ivanka's fashion line is aimed at aspirational young working women. As a result, women are boycotting Ivanka's foreign-made clothing, handbags and shoes as well as the retailers who sell them. Developers no longer want to pay to have the Trump name on their buildings. The Trump brand no longer stood for luxurious and affluent. It now represented darkness, bigotry, sexism, racism and anger. Trump is a billionaire so it's not affecting him financially, but the name will no longer be remembered for its opulence.

"Trump will now be associated with hate."
— *Mr. Genaro*

Farrakhan Demands

"We see how crooked politics lead to corruption; so what is our demand?"

— *Farrakhan*

I want to look at Mrs. Clinton for a minute because my dear brother and sister, this is serious. Her husband and Joe Biden were the authors of THE CRIME BILL that put tens of thousands of black brothers and sisters in prison. So while we were organizing for the Million Man March, they were organizing to put black men and women in jail. Mrs. Clinton backed the crime bill and called young black people "super predators." Of course, she apologized…but just a minute. Hitler could have said to the Jews after Auschwitz, "Ahh, ah I'm sorry." Would that be enough to satisfy you? You couldn't satisfy any Jewish person with an apology. Reparations were demanded for the evil of Adolf Hitler to the Jewish people. What will blacks demand for the evil that has been done to them as a people for 461 years? Mr. Clinton took the safety net out from under welfare recipients. Some welfare mothers were taking advantage of the system [just] like white people, such as Mr. Trump who took advantage of every loop hole in the tax structure. In his debate with Mrs. Clinton he said, "Well if you didn't like that, why didn't you bring up a law when you were in Congress? You could've stopped it." But too many of her friends were using the same loop holes.

This is crooked politics which lead to corruption. The Clintons raised hundreds of millions of dollars; even billions were raised for Haiti after the 2010 earthquake. But no one knows where the money went. It's a mystery but it ain't hard to figure out. Trump knew exactly why he was calling Hillary Clinton "CROOKED HILLARY." It was because Hillary was crooked. Maybe Trump heard what Farrakhan was telling blacks or maybe he didn't but Trump did have something to say to blacks. "If your lifestyle sucks already and as a white billionaire I can only assume it does, why not try something new? To those suffering I say, 'vote for Donald Trump and I will fix it.' What do you have to lose?"

Then he hit blacks below the belt and gave them something t really think about. "There's another civil rights issue we need to talk about and that's the issue of immigration enforcement." He went on to explain how it was also hurting the blacks. "Every time an African-American loses their job to an illegal immigrant, the rights of that American citizen have been violated." Blacks had to look at his way of thinking and realize he was possibly right. "Yes, let's build a wall but let's do it to help African-Americans! It outright meets civil rights! The best cross-over hit since "Walk This Way." Don Whitman, a Trump supporter, agreed with his logic and gave Trump a thumb up. "The Republicans took them out of slavery and were trying to do it again; trying to take them out of enserfment." But blacks didn't believe Trump. They believed he was a bigot and he was just trying to appear like he wasn't a racist. It's been over a year since he was elected the President and Trump hasn't done anything to help blacks; nothing at all.

AMP

American   Money   Publishing

WE PUBLISH THE REALIST BOOKS

Chapter Twenty-eight

Hitler's White House

On the approved list of visitors to see the infamous man, Adolf Hitler, were two men: a German Admiral who was short and stocky, and with him was a tall Austrian Colonel who was privileged to witness the gloomy forest bunker of the man who called himself "The Greatest German" ever. Both had flown in that morning from Berlin. It was a 350 mile journey across the plains of what was once Northern Poland but became a part of the Third Reich. They landed in a remote area close to a little town called Rastenburg; a primeval forest, inserted with lakes and hills. Hitler had a car waiting for their arrival to escort them into the woods along a winding cobblestone road. They were in route to the protected place known as Wolfsschanze—The Wolf's Lair.

To get there they had to go over the railway line, passing many small lakes. Hitler, like Trump, made sure he was heavily protected. For Trump, the Secret Service had to add to their security by securing a wider perimeter for Trump and even paying him for Trump's room when they had to stay in his hotels. The two men were driven through a series of roadblocks with each stop being more terrifying and intimidating than the last which blotted the additional five mile route to the actual headquarters of Adolf Hitler. He recruited nothing but the best once he came into power and security and the military were his first priorities.

Security arrangements were enforced by the S.S., the Führer's Praetorian Guard. Every checkpoint spared no security risk. The black-shirted S.S. soldiers ordered the Admiral and Colonel to show their papers. They were skilled, authoritative and detailed. As they proceeded, there were extensive telephone conversations with higher ranked personnel at each checkpoint. After many security checks and the satisfaction of the guards that everything was in order, the gate was finally raised, giving the visitors the raised arm [Nazi] salute. The two men entered into no-mans-land filled with minefields and pillboxes which made them realize they were in the innermost sanctum of Nazi power. They were surrounded by barbed wire which was electric. It was a fortified encampment of dozens of concrete bunkers and wooden huts that were all camouflaged by thick trees and camouflage nets.

But within this vault of security was another even more guarded place. It was where Hitler actually took refuge; a compound covered with anti-aircraft guns and was continuously patrolled by S.S. men. This was the actual location that contained a bunker where Hitler slept. It was his living quarters which included a single-story, wooden barrack where he would hold his midday conferences while instructing operations against the Soviet Union. Hitler was always masterminding, always preparing for what country he would take over next. He wanted to conquer the world and he hated how America ran its country. It was Hitler's ultimate goal to prove that his way was right and that democracy was wrong. The compound was scary and overshadowed with gloom. It was as if the sun refused to shine in his part of the woods. There were soldiers and barking dogs everywhere with the occasional passing of a train along a nearby railway line.   Mostly, the only sounds heard were the barking of the dogs and the sounds of the forest.

Hitler's staff and soldiers hated the Wolf's Lair. To them it was grim. "It's a cross between a monastery and a concentration camp," said General Alfred Jodl, head of the German armed forces operations staff. Hitler's own architect, Albert Speer said, "The Führer's bunker was like an Egyptian tomb." But for Hitler, it offered him comfort away from the evil threat of the Eastern front and political intrigues of Berlin. He felt safe in the dark forest because he was dark inside. The dark forest removed the outside horrors and created the ideal backdrop for his fierce tirades against the outside world. In the Wolf's Lair, Hitler would spend 800 more days there than at any of his other secured headquarters. The Wolf's Lair was Hitler's White House.

Hitler was a wartime war hero to some, and he was the German dictator who had stunning military success. He accomplished the takeover of Czechoslovakia, the Blitzkrieg attack against Poland and he invaded the Soviet Union. But Hitler became aware of a new enemy that was emerging. It was a country very powerful and whose productive capabilities were so fearsome that they threatened to overwhelm the military might of Nazi Germany. They called her America. And Hitler knew a war with America could possibly cripple Germany. Trump felt the same way about China and Russia and just like Hitler he would soon face a new enemy.

Godlike Aura

Trump had people coming in and out of Trump Towers as he interviewed anybody he felt could be useful to him now that he was the elected President. He appeared to be intrigued by people who had millions or even billions of dollars. It was obvious he felt they were the smartest. He was surrounding himself with what he believed were the smartest people in America. He needed the people who could help him make the best decisions and therefore make him look smarter. Men of power will get other people to make smart decisions and they will take all the credit. A leader has to know how to use the wisdom, intelligence and legwork of people who are masters in their fields in order to be a success at leading. If a man surrounds himself with smart people it will make him look smart and with that type of assistance he can produce world solutions to world problems faster and solve them correctly.

Trump made an intelligent decision to stop companies from hiring people outside the country by proposing the addition of a 35% tax on those businesses who chose to move outside the country. That was a smart move which will help keep employment in America. That type of thinking and action gives him a Godlike aura; as if he can do the unthinkable. The media is asking, "Why didn't Obama do that?" That's a very good question. But Trump is a businessman and he knows business. He knows what can help business and what can hurt business which is why he hit them "below the belt." There are people who represent companies who are saying that it wasn't Trump who created jobs, it was the business. "Trump can't create jobs, only businesses can," a spokesman for a company said. But it doesn't matter what he said. Trump will get the credit and that's all that matters to him. Trump knows the cleverness of hiring someone else to the job that can do it better. He has been doing it all his life. It is a strategy the President has mastered. It gives him a Godlike strength and power.

People were confused by Trump's picks for his Administration. But the man is brilliant and he took his time to make the right choices which will make him a legend to be remembered forever. America has not agreed with all his choices because during his campaign he promised he would not have a government that worked with Wall Street. But he ended up hiring a man who not only works for Wall Street but a guy who made millions of dollars from the exact business issue that crushed American families. He was directly involved in the housing crash. Senator Warren said, "Using Wall Street insiders to run the United States will help a handful of people and leave everybody else behind." She continued, "He tapped into that anger amid at Wall Street insiders then turned around and hired them and put them in powerful positions."

But Trump was unconcerned about what the media was saying; although, he detests humiliation he will do what he pleases and will never apologize for his acts. He also decided to pick Ben Carson as his nominee for Secretary of Housing and Urban Development even though Trump attacked him during the campaign. "How stupid are the people?" Trump asked, referring to Dr. Carson pulling out a knife. But Trump believed that Ben Carson was the best pick for that position. It's simple; learn to put others in positions so they can do the work while the head-man-in-charge takes the credit.

When football teams win, the praise goes to the coach and the owner. It's the same with the presidency. It's a team of men and women. It's an Administration that must be built on having smart people who are masters at what they do. Trump knew the importance of finding people who had the skills he lacked so that their intelligence becomes his and he would appear to look like a genius. Bismarck told all who were listening, "Fools say that they learn by experience. I prefer to profit by others' experience. One man's talent can become another man's talent. His skills can become another's skill. Men of power know this and will use it to further their cause."

Law #7 – The 48 Laws of Power
— Robert Greene

"Get others to do the work for you,
but always take the credit."
— Robert Greene

Chapter Twenty-nine

Only the Beginning

God works in mysterious ways. It is unheard of that a man with so many immoral qualities could actually become the top runner-up for the President of the United States. Trump's greed, fornication, groping, racist character, misogyny and adultery issues were no deterrent. America still saw him as the chosen one. The sad part of it all is that even with all those unsavory characteristics, the mostly white Evangelicals still supported him. Eric Metaxas of the "Wall Street Journal" said, "Trump believed that the Evangelicals obviously felt they had no choice. They must have believed if Hillary Clinton was elected she would've appointed a Supreme Court Justice who would have agreed with her on abominable abortion practices and also crushed America's right to religious freedom."

Metaxas could have been right because it goes against everything the church stands for to back an individual like Trump who seems to have no principals or morals. It would appear that religious leaders are putting at risk all that their moral authority stands for.

Trump is considered grotesque in the eyes of many people. He believes the need for climate control is a hoax after Obama fought so hard for it. "I think that President Obama should apologize for Obama Care," said Trump. After young, white kids kept murdering innocent students in schools all around the country, Trump said, "There will be no gun restrictions on my watch. It is a Constitutional right. We have the right to bear arms." He also said, "Obama founded ISIS and Hillary is the co-founder." He says whatever comes out of his mouth with no facts to prove it. And still his supporters would not budge from their support of Trump. The Bible says, "For what will it profit a man if he gains the entire world and forfeits his soul?"

It's no secret that Trump has exposed the country to the tension and different thought processes among older white men leading the religious right, the younger leaders, women and minorities. Older white men want to outlaw abortion and preserve religion freedom, but the new generation believes it's their obligation to care about immigrants, the poor, refugees and the environment. Trump has opened Pandora's Box and there is no end to the destruction America can soon face. THIS IS ONLY THE BEGINNING!

> *"California and Sacramento*
> *prepares for war against Trump."*
> — *Top Leaders*

As Trump Thinks

The Bible says, "As a man thinketh in his heart, so shall he be." This is a belief that not only embraces the whole of a man's being but is so comprehensive it reaches out to every condition and circumstance of life. Trump is a perfect example of a man who has made his thoughts materialize into his reality. He believed in his thoughts then made them tangible. As he thinks, he becomes. Every man who has become a great man the world will remember has done the same thing. Trump has controlled his destiny just like every other powerful man or woman on this earth. He's already accomplished more than an ordinary person would accomplish in three lifetimes.

It's not about money anymore for Trump. He's accomplished that feat. It's bigger than money. It's about his legacy and what other things he can accomplish before he runs out of time. Every person is literally what they think with their character being the sum total of all their thoughts. People are made or unmade by themselves. Trump is the master of thought, the molder of character and the maker and shaper of his condition. Although many people throughout the world do not agree with Trump or think like him, his way of thinking has made him the most powerful man in the world. He is in control of the United States of America. Its nuclear weapons are now in the HANDS OF TRUMP. He has shaped his environment and destiny.

As a being of power, intelligence, love and the lord of his own thoughts, humans hold the key to every situation. They also contain within themselves that transforming and regenerative agency which Trump used to convert himself into whatever he wills. When humans are in control of their thoughts, they become the masters of their destinies. Every human is anxious to improve their circumstances but many are unwilling to improve themselves. Therefore, they remain bound to their unhappy lifestyle. Trump never shrank from self-crucifixion and a man who doesn't shrink from self-crucifixion can never fail to accomplish the object upon which his heart is set. Every thought-seed sown or allowed to fall into the mind, and to take root there, produces its own thoughts; blossoming sooner or later into action and bearing its own fruit of opportunity and circumstances. This is the thought pattern used by Trump. He turns his thoughts into actions which allow them to blossom. It's like a tree that starts out as a seed but if continually watered will eventually become a tree. Good thoughts bear good fruit and bad thoughts bear bad fruit. People attract what they are, not what they aren't. They may not be able to directly choose their circumstances, but they can CHOOSE THEIR THOUGHTS and therefore indirectly shape their circumstances.

There is no intelligent accomplishment until thought is linked with purpose. With the majority the bark of thought is allowed to "drift" upon the ocean of life. Most people can have strong, powerful thoughts that can change their lives; thoughts that can make them rich, powerful and possibly even the President of the United States. A thought without action is nothing. It produces nothing and it creates nothing. Aimlessness is a vice and such drifting must not continue for the man who would steer clear of catastrophe and destruction. A person must conceive a purpose in their heart and set out to accomplish it. Trump, after accomplishing goal after goal, decided he wanted to become the 45th President of the United States and he set out to accomplish it. He didn't believe it was out of reach and he didn't believe it wasn't possible. He made that goal his supreme focus and devoted himself to attaining it. He never allowed his thoughts to wander off into ephemeral fantasies, longings and imaginings. When he was asked if he thought he could win, he would reply, "I always think I'm gonna win." But even if a man fails again and again to accomplish his purpose, the strength of his character gained will be the measure of his true success.

> *As a man thinketh, so shall he be.*
> — *James Allen*

AMP

American   Money   Publishing

WE PUBLISH THE REALIST BOOKS

Chapter Thirty

Trump vs. Hillary

New York, New York, the Big Apple, Trump and his model wife rode down the escalator inside the luxury lobby of his Fifth Avenue skyscraper —Trump Tower—is where Trump built himself. It was in the month of June during the year 2015 when Donald J. Trump announced to the world that he was entering the race for President of the United States. Hillary Clinton walked onto a stage on an East River island named for one of her political heroes and also announced to the world she was launching her Presidential campaign in earnest in three days and about a mile from Trump Tower. No one was prepared for what happened over the next 18 months. No one took Trump as a serious candidate whereas the world pretty much expected Hillary to run. She was already the assumed

Democrat standard-bearer heading into the 2016 campaign.

For eight years she had been making all the right moves to put herself in the right position to be qualified to become the first woman President of the United States. She had been waiting eight years and in 2016 she believed she was ready and it was her time. But Trump had made no preparations at all. He was like a drunk who stumbled out a bar and just decided that he wanted to run for the next President of the United States. He was an impossible choice, a for-sure loser and a man with no chance of winning. But yet, he launched his campaign. He was the 12th Republican to enter the race; although it was rumored he was once a Democrat. With no political experience, no one expected anything more than reality TV-style entertainment. He was looked upon as a joke, especially after he opened his mouth with his fourth grade vocabulary. But the joke was on America. Trump would outlast every Republican and would end up as the Republican nominee for President. The last week before Election day people could only look back at the clues Trump exposed about why Hillary or his campaign would turn out the way no one predicted.

Clinton's sure win to the White House was almost crushed by Bernie Sanders but she still could have pulled off the victory. And Trump would annihilate his competition of nine past or present Governors and five past or present U.S. Senators easily. Clinton immediately attempted to show the country that she would be the best choice for President. She promised "four fights." She said she wanted to create a much fairer economy, maintain the leadership of America in the world, bring families together in strength, and finally reform government. She revealed her promises at her first huge rally which she held at a park named Roosevelt D. Franklin who, ironically, also promised "four fights" in the war in the year 1941. "I'm a fighter," she told the crowd who listened intently without realizing that she would have to be a fighter because her opponent, Donald Trump, would turn out to be extremely combative. He would challenge her on everything he could think of and never back down from whatever she would throw his way, including his hate for women and sexual assaults. Trump would end up being known as one of the most successful brawlers in the history of U.S. elections.

Donald Trump would enter the race with a totally different approach. He said he wasn't a politician and he didn't act like one. He shocked the world with the words which came out of his mouth. "Mexico sends us the people they don't want. They send us their criminals and rapists. I'm going to send them all back and build a wall," he said. "And I'm going to make Mexico pay for it!" The crowd was stunned but they also felt his pain and they realized that Trump also felt their pain. He was bold, he was crazy, he was outspoken and he was not like other politicians. He was a new breed and people started to listen. He said he would build the wall so high and so long that illegal immigrants would never get over it. He told the people that's what he does, he builds buildings and he would build the wall along the southern border. "Americans don't have victories anymore, especially in trade negotiations," he said. The crowd roared with cheers and applause. "That's also what I do. I make the best deals."

Donald Trump made a promise to the people to make America great again and it was music to their ears. Trump would tap into a new group of people who believed that the billionaire real estate mogul should be their new leader. And for months to come the race would get nasty, denigrating, unsavory and downright ugly. The important men in suits would reveal their true colors. Racism would rise to the forefront and women in dresses would express how they really felt about sexual assault and groping. Trump would keep it simple, especially since most of his supporters were not college graduates and had no love for politicians. He would talk about jobs, the terrible trade deals with China and immigration. But as the months passed he would talk about crime, the dishonesty of lying politicians and rigged elections. He was able to capitalize on the weaknesses of his enemies and opponents. He never elaborated on how he would fix the problems. He would just say, "Believe me," and that appeared to be enough.

American   Money   Publishing

WE PUBLISH THE REALIST BOOKS

Chapter Thirty-one

On the other hand, Hillary continued to stand her ground in the way of the standard politician. She maintained her four goals which appealed to the regular voters and Democrats. She acted like the perfect candidate with no flaws; and each word she spoke sounded like it was group-tested and committee-vetted. She would lay out the details for how she planned to make her four goals emerge. She called for universal prekindergarten for every 4-year old within a decade. On a radio interview she was questioned about Obama's plan to send 450 military advisors to Iraq to be in combat in the Islamic State. She appeared to make sure she would give the best answers possible as she carefully answered, "I do not believe that the U.S. troops should be on the ground in Iraq doing combat. I think what the President is trying to accomplish is using the unique skills that the

American military has in intelligence, surveillance and training to buttress the efforts of the Iraqis themselves.   I have supported the President's approach to dealing with this very serious threat." But when Trump was asked about the same issue, he said, "We should go blast the hell out of that oil!"

Trump did not do anything like the politicians who had run before him. He had no text, no filter and outright refused to read a teleprompter. He said what he wanted to say and had no fear of what his audience or the world thought. He was erratic, mechanical and had a habit of being wordy in speech. But he was also entertaining and forward. "I'm really rich," he would say and then disgracefully talk about his hotels. He would boast, "I built a great business."   But he did not organize his political campaign.   His main tools were using Twitter, Facebook and the media who consistently talked about him because of his outrageous remarks. He said he had one million Facebook fans and three million Twitter followers. He would get on Facebook and Tweet every day.

Clinton would be forced to face tough questions about trade deals. Trump felt trade deals had not been made in the best interest of the people. Although they had developed new areas of economic activity and created new markets for our exports, but they lowered wages for millions of working Americans and banished jobs. Bernie Sanders agreed with Trump on global trading so Hillary began to backtrack on her original stand. She realized that Trump was possibly right and that she was beginning to change how she felt about the unpopular Trans-Pacific Partnership (TPP) and began to convince Obama and House Minority Leader Nancy Pelosi to make sure we get the best, strongest deal possible; and if we don't get that, there should be no deal. But as time passed, Hillary abandoned her support for the agreement completely. Another issue overlooked by Clinton—who also ran for the Presidency in 2008—was the fact that she did not focus on being a woman and would be the first woman President. But in 2016, she seemed to adopt her role as a woman as she joked, "I might not be the youngest person ever elected, but I will be the youngest woman!" Of course Trump responded by accusing her of playing the woman's card. "She's playing the woman card really big," he said. "I watched her the other day and all she would talk about was women! 'I'm a woman! I'm going to be the youngest woman in the White House'!" Then she would show her motherly side by reading *The Very Hungry Caterpillar* to a preschool class. Trump would later make fun of a crying baby. At the end of the day, Trump vs. Hillary was simple:

> *Hillary was stuck in politician mode*
> *and Trump was a realist.*
> *He lived in the real world of white America.*
> — *Patterson*

Trumped-up Immigrants

Trump vowed to send back over three million immigrants once he made it to the White House. "It will be the first thing I will do!" he told the voters. "The criminals and the rapists will be the first ones to go!" Any and all undocumented immigrants would be rounded up in America and deported back to their countries. It would be the first time anything like that would be done in American history. It is estimated that there are 11 million undocumented immigrants in America and about 820,000 of them have been convicted of a crime. However, 300,000 of them were only convicted of a misdemeanor that was considered serious. According to the Department of Homeland Security, it is estimated that 1.9 million immigrants are actually considered "removable criminal aliens." This also included foreigners with legal status; immigrants convicted of any crime except a parking ticket; and those who were repeatedly caught crossing the border. Most of the immigrants were already in custody which meant they wouldn't have to be tracked down and were easily identifiable. They are being housed in federal and state institutions and spread around from city to city in county jails.

As President of the United States there are things Trump can do without Congress or a majority vote. If he wanted to expand the size of immigration and customs enforcement to track down undocumented immigrants he would have to ask Congress. But he does have the power to redirect the current 14,000 "ICE" (U.S. Immigration and Customs Enforcement) officers, agents and special agents to focus on arresting any and all illegal aliens. As of December 2016, there were 1,000 to 1,100 agents assigned to track down illegal immigrants and fugitives who are criminals and gang members, according to the former acting Director of ICE, John Sandweg. The other officers and agents would cover other areas of criminal behavior such as screening visa applicants in foreign countries;

detention operations; immigration audits of U.S. businesses; and investigating money laundering and human trafficking. But the President can tell the Director to do as he wishes. There is complete flexibility for the Director of ICE to redirect his agents to track down illegal immigrants if that's what Trump wanted him to do.

When an illegal immigrant is captured, before deportation, they must appear before a judge where they are allowed a hearing. But most courts are overburdened and extremely behind. In 2016, it was reported that the backlog was up to 52,676 cases which meant it would take almost two years before those cases could be heard and a decision made. If Trump wanted to speed up the process—which averaged about 700 to 1,000 days a case—more judges would need to be hired and that would require him to go through Congress. And even if Trump's request to hire more judges was approved, it would take almost six years to accomplish his goal. And he ran the risk of not being re-elected for President.

But in January 2017, Trump will have wide discretion toward enforcing the immigration laws that was a part of his signature campaign promise. He vowed to seal the border against terrorists, criminals and millions of people trying to enter the United States illegally. And he promised to send those already in the United States back. And since immigration tapped into sovereignty, the discretion is almost entirely up to Trump. "I will emphasize criminals before deciding about law-abiding families legally in the country," Trump told the CBS TV news show "60 Minutes." The Executive Director of The National Immigration Forum, Ali Noorani said, "Trump doesn't need any new money to change the focus of the immigration agents who are already in place. If the Department of Homeland Security Secretary green lights, simply in tone, the ramping up of enforcement actions, that is a system that can wreak havoc very, very quickly."

If Trump focuses on criminals first, it may leave millions of other undocumented immigrants safe from wrath, such as the group Obama created under the Deferred Action for Childhood Arrivals program (DACA). At least 800,000 young undocumented immigrants have sought approval with the program which is designed to protect them from deportation for two-year periods and grants them work permits. But Trump has the power to revoke each and every DACA case. To qualify, all that was needed was to register with the federal government, have no criminal record and either work or go to school. Trump had already said he would eradicate the program and rescind their deportation protections which have immigrants living in fear. The program was initiated by an Executive Memorandum by Obama's Secretary of Homeland Security. So, Trump's Secretary could easily abolish the memo and/or issue a new updated one.

Trump could also revoke their work permits but it would be more complicated because of U.S. law. Homeland Security is required to provide a written notice and immigrants would have 15 days to respond. It would be effective but it would be much slower. Therefore, it's plausible that Trump go after the immigrants with no criminal record first. After all, it is the unpredictable Donald Trump who does have the power and he will not hesitate to use it. Or abuse it.

Chapter Thirty-two

Trumped-up Muslim Ban

"I'm calling for a temporary ban on all immigrants from all Muslim countries," Trump said. The question is: could he actually do it? He attempted to lay out a plan on how he would do it. "I will target immigrants from 'terror-prone regions' where vetting cannot safely occur." It is possible that Trump could possibly do it if he worded such a proclamation based on terrorism grounds and not religious grounds," said Legomsky. But if he approached the ban based on religion, it was possible that he could've been bombarded with lawsuits from several groups with complaints of violating 1st Amendment protections for freedom and religion. Presidents do not have power like a dictator, but they do have power, including the power to forbid access into the United States for specific immigrants or entire classes of immigrants.

The guidelines for that power is outlined in the Immigration and Nationality Act which gives Presidents discretion to block would-be immigrants who are perceived as "harmful" to the interests of the United States. Trump believes that he can utilize that discretion, although the provision has never been applied in the way he would like to see it. It has rarely been used over the past decades and when it was used it was mainly for dictators, military strongmen, or anyone who attempted to undermine democracy in countries like South Sudan, North Korea, Libya and Venezuela. However, America has never used it the way Trump said he would implement it, in American history. But America hasn't done a lot of things until the rise of Trump.

"Man looks to himself for what he does not find in others, and to others what he has too much of himself."
— *Malcolm de Chazal*

Refugees to Zero

Once Trump realized the extent of his power to change the number for 110,000 refugees to zero, it was very likely that's what he would do. "Congress can ask questions and object to things, but ultimately it's up to the President," said Stephen Legomsky, Professor Emeritus at Washington University School of Law. The President's power reaches a long way with unilateral prudence in determining which refugees fleeing from war or other threats from their countries to safety are allowed to enter the United States. He has the choice to "just say no." The United States was accepting refugees every year and it's the President who decides that number. Before President Obama, that number was 70,000 per year in 2015, Obama raised the number to 110,000 in 2017. But the refugees would never enter America in those numbers. They would never make it to America because Trump would become the new President.

Before he became President he battered Obama's decision to raise the number to 110,000. Trump did not want any refugees, Muslims or any kind of immigrants coming into the United States. "Refugee countries like Syria are a threat to national security because they are not properly vetted and can include terrorists," Trump stated, although the

State Department said otherwise. They said Syrian refugees undergo the strictest background checks. But that information fell on deaf ears because Trump had intentions of dropping that number to ZERO.

The President

"WE'RE GOING IN THE WRONG DIRECTION. DONALD TRUMP HAS A CHANCE TO CHANGE THAT. HE'S THE ONLY HOPE THE COUNTRY HAS."

On November 8, 2016, Donald J. Trump was victorious over expected Democratic winner Hillary Clinton. She won the popular [people] vote. Trump became President by a landslide through the Electoral College process.

DONALD J. TRUMP
THE UNITED STATES 45TH PRESIDENT

Trump has accomplished his greatest feat yet, but it's still a rush for him to stand in Trump Towers and look out the windows of his lavish penthouse that's 600 feet above ground. He looks down at the world as if he is God himself. The people walking around down below resemble ants hard at work as they walk to and from work, getting in and out of cars that look like toys on a racetrack. The huge ice skating rink in Central Park looks like a miniature model. Only the elite ever have the luxury of experiencing that view. You have to make it to the 66th, 67th and 68th floors which most regular people will never see unless they are an important part of the staff or his secret service. Trump calls the 66th, 67th and 68th floors in Trump Towers his home. Hired staff members are required to wear cloth coverings over their shoes because the majority of the floors are marble and the plush carpeting is very expensive. Trump's Secret Service tries to avoid the marble floors and take their chances on the carpeting, hoping they won't stain it.

The new President of the United States lives an extraordinary life with antique clocks and art painted as murals on the high ceilings which included gym rat Greek Gods. The name Trump is embossed on napkins and the Trump shield embroidered on pillows. It's not uncommon to see planes flying outside his windows or other skyscrapers which contain the money of other billionaires. There is no green grass or community in the sky; no postman or cars parked out front; no picket fence or long driveway. Trump almost lives in the clouds. Crystal is usually hanging above his head as he walks from one room to another with diamond cufflinks at his wrists. Although the hired staff must wear coverings over their shoes, the Secret Service and Trump and his family do not. But they do try to avoid scuffing the marble floors.

Sometimes it's even hard for the Secret Service to believe it really did happen. No one expected Donald Trump to win the Presidency. But it really did happen and it's their job to protect him. They must now put their lives on the line for the man people consider a racist, narcissistic, vulgar, a showoff and a sexist. But he is also that man who now represents the forefront of America and he did it by grabbing the front page headlines of newspapers, magazines, tabloids, etc. because of all his negative titles. He is the leader and in control of the world's most lethal military and economic levers that can affect billions of lives.

And Trump always wins. He knows how to win and he always finds a way to win. This time he found it through the people the nation had left behind. But Trump remembered them. They were the union workers, the mine workers and the ones who knew nothing about technology but they knew about hard work. How is it that a billionaire remembered the poor and made a decision to voice his concern? He had an abnormal approach but it was his distasteful qualities which gave him strength. He remembers his fight as he sits down at his marble desk under his two-story ceiling. There were times when it looked bad and Trump had to make changes but he was never a quitter. He had run into many snags over his lifetime but he always prevailed and he knew all he had to do was fix his problems. Now that he was President he would have the power to fix almost any problem he felt was a problem. His powers are almost unlimited in foreign affairs. He can give an order and thousands of troops will engage in combat. He has the power to bomb any country. He can have agents and officers round up immigrants. He can listen in on his potential enemies and spy on millions of people across the world.

Many people felt that Trump was unfit to be President. Now the world is waiting to find out. He hasn't appointed people who will stand up to him. Plus, the world feels he possibly won't live up to his campaign promises. Trump could become a successful President if he behaved less erratically, especially during his campaign. The most caustic, Presidential campaign in memory ended with amplified division among gender, ethnicity and education. Coalitions were formed for each major party whose voices could resonate in American politics for a generation. There was no doubt that Trump had inherited division in America. "Being the President is big business. Running the Trump Organization is peanuts compared to being the President. Forget my businesses, AMERICA NEEDS ME RIGHT NOW," Trump said.

His unorthodox approach to the Presidency will forever be remembered. He entered the race like no other politician in history and he did it with disobedient genius. While Hillary painted the picture of a bright vision for America, Trump did the opposite. He painted a picture of a dark America we were all living in. He created hidden levels of fear and anger that resided within the country. As its been mentioned earlier in this book, some can call him stupid and some might call him a genius, but no matter your analysis of Donald Trump, it is undeniable that he gravitated toward issues others did not realize existed. He was able to prevail with the ultimate art of the deal.

Everything that seemed to be against him was actually working in his favor. The late night comedians that constantly mocked him and defamed his character night after night; the "National Press," "Fox News" and "CNN" whose reports were always negative about the real estate mogul President; the elected leaders who believed he was an embarrassment to America and its political agenda; the donors who took flak from their peers and every one of the Americans who called him racist and sexist. They all believed he was a joke and could never imagine that one day he would become their President. But Trump reinvented the game, the same way he did with his first business venture when he built the Grand Hyatt Hotel near Grand Central Station. Whenever it appeared as if Trump was at his worst, he was at his best. Just as he built his first skyscraper, he's now building his legacy. He made pollsters look like blockheads. The demagogue puzzled the country with more Latino and male African-American votes than the 2012 Republican nominee. His way was obviously the best way for the recipe for politics.

"The greatest jobs theft in the history of the world" was his movement. "I alone can fix it!"
— Donald Trump

American   Money   Publishing

WE PUBLISH THE REALIST BOOKS

Chapter Thirty-three

Trumped Hillary Out

The real estate mogul scored big on November 8, 2016, as he left dirt in the faces of Hillary Clinton and the Democratic Party. Nobody was partying except Trump and his supporters. He was expected to lose in Florida but, surprisingly, he was not only victorious in Florida but he won in Ohio, too. The early results shocked voters, viewers, pollsters and flustered investors. The Dow futures fell hard to 600 points. The market was in a panic about the uncertainty of a Trump Administration. Although his leads in Georgia and North Carolina were close, he was able to pull it off. The thin line of votes chased an equally divisive 2016 Presidential campaign that would have an enormous impact on continuing or eradicating the policies of President Obama.

The turnout was clear as Trump jumped out front as if he was Bugs Bunny racing the cartoon turtle. Hillary Clinton would have been the first woman President after 228 years of men. But the real-estate-mogul-reality-TV-star had taken a gamble and it was looking as if though he would hit the jackpot. Trump would be unlike any President America had ever encountered. He was a billionaire, he had no political experience, he had a flashy style and he was "full" of himself. If elected, he would reinvent the word President. History was in the making and the Trump campaign was feeling it. It was all over their faces and in their conversation. The votes were not yet in but CNN and Fox News were giving blow-by-blow reports of the numbers and who looked good and who didn't. Trump appeared to be on top in most of the states; the states expected and unexpected.

But Hillary supporters were in for the shock of their lives. They were banking on a completely different turnout. CNN was saying, "If Hillary wins Florida, it's pretty much over for Trump." But that didn't happen and the number of women that showed up wearing pantsuits, as if a woman could put on pants just like a man and fit in the shoes of a man, was astounding. It was also written all over their faces. But if Hillary had won, history definitely would have been made and that knowledge hung in the air until the day dwindled away. They were paying homage to the woman who would become the first woman President ever. Hundreds of women made a pilgrimage to a Rochester, New York cemetery where the headstone of Susan B. Anthony remains to show their respect and honor the leader whose work paved the way for women to have the right to vote. They plastered "I VOTED" stickers on her headstone but it would be to no avail because Hillary would not win. She came so close but yet was so far away.

She ran a barrier breaking campaign that took place almost a century later but it would fall short of victory. Instead, it was loud-mouthed Trump with his insults, barrage of Tweets, sexist acts, racist attributes and disrespect of the disabled and war heroes who would achieve greatness at the end of the day. Trump had the last laugh. He would say he was not politically correct as his excuse for bad behavior and his supporters would agree. They had his back like a wife would for her husband. Trump and his supporters became married to the game. Indeed, it was an election whose ultimate decision was decided based on character as well as issues.

But it was Trump who threw the "money Mayweather punch" when he tapped into the anger of the people. Although a lot of people were distracted by Clinton's email scandal which emerged again in the final 11 days of the campaign, they were also bothered by Trump's treatment of women. It was all his issues which tipped him overboard. It was his issues that made voters feel they'd rather Hillary walk the plank and keep Trump on board.

It's no doubt the F.B.I. played a major part in the voters' decisions because the majority of voters made up their minds during the last few days when Hillary's email scandal was resurfaced by F.B.I. Director Comey and plastered all over the TV, as if Trump paid them to do so. The on again-off again investigation into Hillary's emails was devastating and unsavory. The majority felt it actually prevented Hillary from becoming the nation's first woman President. Hillary was expected to get a huge boost from the Hispanic and black voters but blacks hadn't forgotten that Bill Clinton signed that Violent Crime Control and Law Enforcement Act of 1994 which included the Three Strikes and You're Out Statute proved to be a war on blacks and resulted in the incarceration of hundreds of thousands of male blacks for a minimum of 15 years to life and in many cases for non-violent crimes. Although she apologized, Hillary lost her trust among blacks.

Trump was propelled to victory by the voters who were frustrated and angry about the direction the country was heading. Trump had gassed up and fueled those who were upset and had plenty of fuel which would take him all the way to the finish line. He didn't do it with cash or class but he did it. And if ugliness is what it took, ugliness is what they got. Trump and the Clintons showed up to cast their votes. Both wore solid blue-New York State suits on that Tuesday, November 8, 2016, morning. Bill and Hillary showed up and there were a crowd of voters who applauded them at her polling place in Chappaqua, New York. Whereas Trump cast his vote in Manhattan where he snuck a peek at his wife, Melania's, vote to make sure she was being loyal to his cause and movement. When he was asked who he voted for, the charming Trump said, "Tough decision."

Ninety million Americans voted that day. They lined up at schools, churches, public libraries, civic centers and anywhere you could officially cast votes. Trump had protested that the polls could be rigged so they were being watched by poll watchdogs and other national observers who monitored the voting.

People were fearful that their votes could be tampered with and hoped for the best. The nation wondered if the votes would be tallied correctly. There were more Hillary voters than Trump but in the end Trump would win big through the Electoral College vote and become the President-elect. The world would be in shock but it wouldn't be the first time Trump would shock them. He had already done it many times before.

AMP

American   Money   Publishing

WE PUBLISH THE REALIST BOOKS

Chapter Thirty-four

Europe Agrees with Trump

As the West gets ready for their up and coming elections, right-wing parties have a stronger belief after seeing how the Trump victory played out. They have also taken a stand against trade deals and immigration. And now with the victory of Trump it is now more believable that they, too, can propel to power. A wave of populism was already spreading to Eastern Europe, cultivating Hungary, Slovenia and Poland with rightist governments. Europe was expected to elect their first far-right head of state since World War II. The Freedom Party's, Norbert Hofer, came very close to losing the race for a ceremonial post in April 2016. But because alleged irregularities in counting the mailed-in ballots a new election was ordered.

Donald Trump's win had the other countries feeling jubilant and excited because lately, countries such as Germany, France and The Netherlands have acquired a U.S. style shift in support from mainstream parties to anti-establishment nationalists. Just as in the United States they complain of weak job prospects linked to globalization; a migrant crisis looked upon as a threat to security; and a fatigue in social benefits. The Europeans are upset about the free flow of labor and migration into the 28 nation bloc. "People are sick and tired of politicians who refused to listen to their worries about rising immigration, the loss of law and order, taxes being spent abroad while domestic needs are rising and trade agreements that harm employment at home," a Dutch lawmaker and leader of The Netherlands Far-Right Party of Freedom said. "We are witnessing a patriotic spring in America as well as Europe," he told "USA Today." "Our people have the same worries as the American people. The Trump victory proves that change is possible."

The Anti-Christ

"Repeatedly, God warns that the day will come when He will bring an end to the world."

Christ is not an evil genius, although it's possible Donald Trump could be. God has repeatedly warned the mother of earth that a man may rise as the man who has all the answers to everyone's problems with no regard to who it might hurt. God is a holy, righteous God. He is great in mercy and compassion and that's been proven in the 13,000 years that the earth has existed. God is the creator of mankind. However, when a man is in power and shows no compassion or empathy, he is not Godlike. The Almighty has been demonstrating his tremendous mercy in this sinful world. But God, in his perfect righteousness, must carry out his laws (as set forth in the Bible) to bring to justice all of mankind who are guilty of sin (Exodus 34:6-7).

The Bible says Christ weeps in sorrow over the fact that he must bring judgment. He derives no pleasure in the death of the wicked. (Ezekiel 33:11). But, when the time of punishment comes, there will not, there cannot be any pity or mercy. God must faithfully and righteously bring to trial and sentence to hell each and every person who is guilty; everyone who is not a genuinely "saved" child of God is going to be caught in the net of the wrath of God. They will receive a blow that is far more terrible than being destroyed by a nuclear weapon; the same type of weapons that rest at the fingertips of Donald Trump. There is no need to rehash all the sinful things Trump has been accused of.

This portion of the book is clearly to point out that God sees all and that even if Trump is smart enough to fool enough people to be voted in as the 45th U.S. President, he can never fool God, the ruler and creator of all mankind and animals. "Each and every unsaved person will be caught and will face judgment." The sun may appear to shine at this moment but when the time comes, which is sooner than any person might know, it will be too late for salvation. Those who don't pass God's judgment will end up eternally under the wrath of God; under eternal damnation (Revelation 20:12-15). There is nothing worse than that. It is terror and that is indescribable in its horror. Our present knowledge of terror becomes completely insignificant in comparison to this unexplainable terror that is fast approaching.

*"The world has violently been
introduced into an age of terror."*

"Time has an end."

A New Power

Donald Trump can't help but see New York's Central Park outside the windows of Trump Towers and is not steadily reminded of his success as he looks at the public ice rink the city government had spent a little over six years and 12 million dollars trying, but failing, to repair. Other real estate developers saw the ice rink as one big waste of money and time. But Trump saw it as a huge opportunity, not just for himself but for the city as well. It was the year 1986 when the young, flashy newcomer in New York real estate made an offer to fix the rink in six months and at his own expense. Like always, Trump was bold, magnanimous and sure of himself. He pointed out, to Mayor Ed Koch, that the incompetence the city had demonstrated with the rink project had to be one of the great embarrassments of his Administration. Trump got the job and he did what he said he would do. He completed it two months ahead of the due date and $800,000 dollars under budget. The city dished out the money but Trump put his name all over it and enjoyed months of the media glorifying him. He was the real estate king who came in and saved the day and this feat became the bedrock of the Trump myths.

The carefully polished billionaire built lavish buildings by smashing through the rules and doing things his way. Because of the Presidency he has been forced to leave his opulent skyscraper on Fifth Avenue to much smaller and less plush quarters in northwest Washington, DC. He is considered the most unusual President America has ever elected to lead the nation. He is a man who has used controversy and confrontation to get what he wants. He is a salesman and a master at marketing but not a diplomat or bureaucratic manager. He never backed down from the establishment types who often laughed at him. It was believed that the new President would lead in much the same ways he was accustomed to doing in business for four decades as a man under his own brand.

"All publicity is good publicity and victory comes to those who fight back a hundred times harder than any hit they might absorb."
— Roy Cohn
Trump's infamous Manhattan lawyer

He won fame and sometimes fortune by putting himself center-stage in all his enterprises.

> *"The show is Trump and it sold-out performances everywhere."*
> — *Donald J. Trump*

The show Trump referred to himself as is a ratings machine, although he is really a loner who has few, if any, close friends. He usually leaves social events alone and as quickly as possible he likes to return to his lavish skyscraper and watch TV by himself, and usually into the wee hours of the night. He believes his company is his best company.

"In public, though, Trump is all business and all show, blending the two in ways that have now shattered the boundary between politics and celebrity."

NO...ON A WOMAN
PRESIDENT,
NOT NOW...POSSIBLY
NOT EVER...

Chapter Thirty-five

America Says No

Hillary Clinton was at one time a highly respected woman and throughout her climb to the top of the political world she's had some trials and tribulations. Her misfortunes required her to build up a shield of protection. For many years she has been attacked on her decisions, her judgment, her marriage, her looks and her motivations which have kept her on the defense. All of these are elements which can harden a once good person and bring out the darker side in them. It is believed that is what happened to Hillary Clinton which possibly caused her to make her most damaging mistakes. She was once named the "most admired woman in the country" a record 20 times by Gallup Poll. She received the annual honor 14 consecutive times.

She rose from a New York Senator to Secretary of State with a 60% public approval rating. But with the armor she created to protect herself, her ratings would begin to crumble. Her downfall would begin as she threw herself into the Presidential race for the second, and most likely last time to become the first woman President of the United States. Unfortunately she did not realize that a large fraction of America did not want a woman President. The feeling was that the Presidency was designed for a man and to have a woman running the country would make America look weak. Now, Trump said a lot of distasteful things but the men in power would not publicly and blatantly express those thoughts to the world. But you better believe, that is how the elite men of America feel, too. Clinton ran a strong, hard race going toe-to-toe and blow-for-blow with Trump. But in the end she would hit the pavement—knocked out cold.

There is no doubt Clinton has thrown in the towel and has run her last race for the White House. Because of Hillary Clinton the next woman who decides to become a candidate for President should easily win a debate, have a strong chance at the primary, become a nominee or win the popular vote. They will know how to get there and will know that a woman has made it that far already. She has carved out a path for the American public to actually believe that a woman President is impossible. Hillary has shown the world that millions of people will vote for a woman President. Because of Hillary Clinton women began to believe that it could possibly happen. "I thought, oh, when Hillary becomes President, girls will be treated better," said a young girl who was also attending the election in New York City. But Hillary's loss also created mixed emotions from different women. "I thought it was really going to happen. It was unbelievable," a Clinton supporter said. But to some it was looked at as another failure and still to others, a setback for women. "Hillary did everything right. She checked all the boxes and clearly that doesn't really win," said Ramsini, an attorney. "If a woman can't beat this guy, then who can she beat?" Hillary could have broken the glass ceiling. But it will possibly be another 200 years before a woman becomes the President of the United States. America says no...and no means no!

Monopolization

Donald Trump was a mastermind at monopolizing his business. If he wasn't building his own buildings, he was somehow involved in the building of other buildings. He also wanted to be involved in any and everything else. He was even a team owner. In 1983, Trump took a large sum of his money and purchased the New Jersey Generals of the United States Football League (USFL). They were an up and coming professional league with a goal to compete with the long, well established National Football League (NFL). Donald loved to win and he hated to lose. He also loved and wanted to compete on the big stage. His team was winners in their field of competition. In 1984 and 1985 they accomplished strong records and winning seasons. Trump, as always, wanted more. With his celebrity status he worked to bring attention to the team and the league. But the team would only play during the spring and Trump was not feeling that. He was a big game player and he wanted to be in the big league.

So he approached the owners of the other teams and convinced them that they should play their league games in the fall and compete directly with the NFL. The league would end up suspending play prior to the 1986 season. For this, Trump would receive criticism. But criticism means nothing to Trump. He received criticism for the people he picked to be a part of his team in the White House. But as said before, Trump is no fool. He is a brilliant businessman which is why he selected CEO's and business owners of billion dollar businesses to work in his Administration. If Trump hires all the big players, he would truly have the world in his hands. He would have more power than he's ever had. Trump was putting himself in a position to know every move all big businesses make so he could create the laws that would be favorable for businesses. Trump has put himself in a position to legally monopolize the game.

"Trump is truly big business."

Still Unpredictable

Being unpredictable can be a valuable tool for success as discussed earlier in this book. Trump knew the value of being unpredictable. He used it while running for President and he's using it now that he is President. He's like a professional poker player who never reveals his hand; never gives away his thoughts through his facial expressions and when he talks it doesn't always make sense. He leaves his supporters who voted for him and the political world guessing and wondering will he do as he promised. And if not, what will he do? Once he became President-elect he didn't immediately explain to the world how he would separate himself from his conflict with the Trump Organization. He wouldn't tip his hand on whether he decided to let his children take the empire over; who were still doing business with foreign countries. He was supporting a broad policy platform in Congress which was shared by Conservatives: a reduction in regulations; he would not fight the global warming issue that he once vowed to fight against; the biggest tax-reduction since Reagan; and a Cabinet filled with free-market philosophers. He has backed off his campaign promise that he would give a huge net tax windfall to the wealthiest according to former Sachs banker, Steve Mnuchin.

Then Trump appeared to back-slide on almost everything he had campaigned on. It was like he was transforming into just another lying politician after securing his position. Trump is a master at confusing people. He called former President George W. Bush's Iraq war fight a disaster after publicly saying he supported the war. He could be extremely contradicting. After promising to reward conservative ideologies with a Supreme Court Justice to their liking, he turns around and rejects a social conservative campaign to keep transgender people out of bathrooms they chose to use. When it came to immigrants he said, "As for the people who were brought to the U.S. illegally as youths and now have work visas under Obama, I would like to find some future accommodation for them." So he was still considering reversing Obama's Executive Order. "We're going to work something out that's going to make people happy and proud," he tells "Time Magazine." "They were brought here at a very young age, they've worked here and they've gone to school here. Some were good students. Some have wonderful jobs. And they're in never-never land because they don't know what's going to happen."

So when it comes to Donald J. Trump the country could be in for a bumpy ride because it appears that even Trump didn't know what he was going to do about certain issues. He said he would terminate the deal made with Obama and Cuba unless multiple demands were met. If Cuba was unwilling to make a better deal for the Cuban people and American-Cuban people, Trump threatened to eradicate the Agreement. Once Trump tried to do business in Cuba and get around the embargo but he was unsuccessful. The world is confused about the Trump millionaire and billionaire club he is surrounding himself with in his Cabinet. They say it's like gators in a swamp. He told Muslims, "They are vile and there's a new sheriff in town and his name is Donald Trump." He has claimed there's a massive voter fraud but he offered no proof. "He's a scared man who thinks someone will take it all away from him," Attorney Strom said. The truth is, no one can predict what's going to happen because the man is too unpredictable.

"Hopefully we can take some of the drama out."
— *Donald Trump*

One thing that has been reported is, Trump lives in fear of being poisoned which is why he eats at McDonalds; not because he has the same name as the franchise, but because the food is pre-prepared and they don't know when he's going to place an order. It has also been reported that he will not let the White House staff touch his toothbrush. So even though he appears fearless, he does live in fear of being assassinated.

WHITE GENOCIDE...
MAKE AMERICA WHITE
AGAIN...

Chapter Thirty-six

Racist Acts...Follow

After the world witnessed Trump win the election and become President-elect, it released a backlash from people who had hidden their racial hatred for years, decades and perhaps a century. They believed that Trump would become the elected President and they could finally unleash their hatred without fear of being judged. They felt safe to openly display their true feelings. Experts and educators said an alarming succession of racist behavior, graffiti signs and crime since Election Day can be linked to Trump's victory. "People looked at the way protesters were manhandled at Trump's rallies and they think, 'oh, if someone disagrees with us we can do those things as well'," said Carlos Wiley, Director of the Paul Robeson Cultural Center at Penn State University. Experts said Trump could have played a crucial role in curbing the disquieting conduct. But Enid Logan who teaches sociology and African-American studies at the University of Minnesota said, "Trump's victory legitimized white supremacists' point of view." In Texas someone was distributing ominous, threatening fliers and posting them around the campus of Texas State University. Their flier read:

"Now that our man Trump is elected
and Republicans own both the
Senate and the House — time to organize tar
and feather vigilante
squads and go arrest and torture
those deviant University
leaders spouting off all this diversity garbage."

The fliers were found in the bathrooms all throughout the campus which quickly spread on social media. The fliers also displayed a group of men clad in camouflage with rifles in their hands and they said diversity was a code word for "WHITE GENOCIDE." A white swastika was scrawled on a wall in a park in Wellsville, New York. It read:

"MAKE AMERICA WHITE AGAIN"

Another message was scrawled in a bathroom in Maple Grove, Minnesota at a high school. It read:

"GO BACK TO AFRICA," "WHITES ONLY" and "WHITE AMERICA" along with "TRUMP TRAIN"

"It looks like America is in for a long ride."
— *Mr. Genaro*

Making His Mark

After being sworn in as the 45th United States President, Donald Trump catapulted his Presidency with a burst of Executive Orders. In his first 30 days he had done more than any President in history. He immediately pulled America out of a major trade Agreement. He also ordered the construction of the Mexican border wall as he promised voters he would. And Trump began the process of dismantling the Affordable Care Act. America was still divided and still in disbelief that Trump had actually won the Presidency. After his inauguration, his first full day in office was blemished by a massive protest of women who were against his Administration and policies for women, and his irate reaction to the media reports about the modest size of his inauguration crowd, unlike previous Presidents.

But that didn't stop Trump's thunder and he wasted no time utilizing his executive pen. He quickly pulled the United States out of the Trans-Pacific Partnership (TPP), a 12-nation trade deal negotiated by the former President Administration which hadn't been ratified by Congress. He scheduled meetings with the Premier of Canada and President of Mexico to begin renegotiating the North American Free Trade Agreement (NAFTA). Trump came out the gate swinging and he didn't care about his approval rating which was barely above 40%. He directed the Department of Homeland Security to start constructing the new border wall and to strip funding for all so-called sanctuary cities that refused to turn over undocumented immigrants to federal authorities.

"Beginning today, the United States of America gets back control of its borders."
— President Trump

Trump wasn't done. He also signed other Executive Orders, such as he directed federal agencies to "waive, defer, grant exemption or delay" any parts of the Affordable Care Act that they deemed burdensome. He cleared the way for the approval of the controversial Keystone XL and Dakota Access oil pipelines that were halted amid environmental concerns. He reinstated the so-called Mexico City Policy regarding U.S. aid for advice, promotion or performing of abortions overseas. He implemented a hiring freeze on all federal government workers except military personnel. His Administration also instructed the Environmental Protection Agency to freeze all of its grants and contracts. And, he also temporarily banned refugees and immigrants from Syria, Iraq, Iran, Libya, Somalia, Sudan and Yemen.

"Without the U.S., the TPP's remaining
11 nations will likely
join a rival trade group that puts
China at its center."

AMP

American   Money   Publishing

WE PUBLISH THE REALIST BOOKS

Chapter Thirty-seven

The Panic

After announcing the ban would be a start to cracking down on immigration, the panic set in before the raids even embarked. Men, women and children were confused about their future. In Cleveland, undocumented women started asking local activists if there was any type of paperwork they could fill out that would protect their children if they got deported. In Brownsville, Texas people were grabbing what they could, leaving their homes and returning back to Mexico.

"Every knock at the door became an occasion for alarm; the fear controlled my body."
— *Zuleima Dominguez*

Zuleima was living in fear although her parents and her brother were documented. "I start crying. I start getting anxiety," she said, expressing her fear. But Trump knew what he was doing. It was all a part of the plan. He wanted them to panic. He wanted them to become afraid and run. The raids that were being enforced by federal officials began on February 4, 2017 and they have then incarcerated 680 people in 12 states. But since then the numbers continue to rise.

"The goal was simply to enforce the laws on the books."
— *Government Agency*

It was reported that about 75% of those arrested had criminal records and convictions and Trump based his actions on his campaign promise:

"Gang members, drug dealers and others are being removed."
— *Trump*

But they were not the only ones. Trump knew exactly what he was doing. He wanted America to return to being white and he would deal with the blacks later. While the previous Administration also conducted raids which included sweeping roundups, those raids focused on specific targets in the immigrant communities. President Obama instructed officials to prioritize and go after hardened criminals only and they would be the ones deported. But this did not happen under the Trump Administration. His Executive Order instructed law enforcement agencies to widen the net and bring them in. His deportable offenses were acts that might warrant future criminal charges which meant they did not have to be a criminal yet. Trump's plan was to track down and apprehend 8 million of the 11 million undocumented immigrants that lived in the U.S. ICE (Immigration and Customs Enforcement) was in full effect as they kicked down doors across the country. But the data from ICE revealed that a lot of the immigrants caught up in the raids did not have any prior convictions.

"The Administration has left entire immigrant communities feeling vulnerable. It pretty much incorporates everyone."
— *Attorney Andre Segura*

Trump's execution on the raids has similar roots from the 1950's. In a December interview in 2015, when he was just a candidate, Trump told "Time" why he had praised Operation Wetback, which was a very controversial deportation program instituted by President Dwight Eisenhower. At that time it was reported that over one million people left the U.S. during the extreme sweep and roundups. But most of them departed on their own rather than being forcibly removed.

"That's proof of the program's success."
— Trump
"Once they knew the country was getting tough on illegal immigration, they left," Trump said.
"They saw what was going on, and they left."
— Trump

But Trump was secretly following the same pattern as Adolf Hitler. He had officers and agents instead of the military, knocking on doors and taking people out of their homes. They were being arrested for being Mexicans, just as Hitler targeted the Jews. They were being rounded up all across the nation and there was nothing anyone could do.

Trump was in power and just like Hitler he set out to get rid of the people he despised.

"Chaos often breeds life. Order breeds habit."
— *Henry Brooks Adams*

Combat Death

Trump's first combat as President kills Anwar Al-Awiaki's daughter. Al-Awiaki was a U.S. born Jhadist who was assassinated by the Obama Administration in a drone strike. The U.S. sent in special U.S. forces to capture intelligence from an Al Qaida compound in Yemen which deteriorated into a chaotic firefight that caused two Americans their lives. It was the first counterterrorism mission ordered by Trump since his Presidency. For that same mission, former President Obama decided it was too risky and he rejected the mission. Pentagon officials reported that U.S. forces were attacked with intense fire when they descended on the village of Yakla. They had to call in the helicopter's gunships and Harrier jets to pound the militants. Things did not go smoothly as chaos erupted. A 70 million dollar Osprey aircraft crashed during the mission. The soldiers had to quickly bomb it to keep it from falling into the hands of the enemy.

"The operation killed 16 civilians, including Nawar, Al-Awiaki's daughter who once inspired and led ISIS."

Yemen has declared:

"No more raids by the U.S."

Yemen has withdrawn permission for the United States to pursue special operations anti-terrorism missions in their country after the carnage left by the U.S. raid. The American raid which was supposed to target a suspected Al-Qaida hideout evolved into a 50 minute firefight that unfortunately killed numerous civilians. The photos were gruesome, displaying several children who were killed in the raid at Yakla. It caused outrage in Yemen. The ultimate target was supposed to have been Qassim Al-Rimi, the leader of Al Qaida's Yemen Branch. Rimi released a recording taunting Trump:

"The new fool of the White House received
a painful slap across his face."

— *Rimi*

The Pentagon and the White House stated that the mission's purpose was to gather intelligence not to hunt down and kill Qassim Al-Rimi and that it was a success. But Trump wouldn't stop there. He was determined to outdo the former black President Barack Obama and he continued his assault on ISIS, vowing to annihilate the terrorist group which proved successful a year later when he would confess he had taken close to 100% of their territory.   But the question remains: who could actually believe Donald Trump? The man tells lies.

Chapter Thirty-eight

Money for the Wall

Trump urged Republican lawmakers to use U.S. taxpayer money to quickly move ahead with building a southern border wall, and convinced them that Mexico would eventually be forced to pay it all back.

> *"We're going to get reimbursed."*
>
> — *Trump*

He convinced them that he didn't want to wait but if they would start they would get reimbursed. Trump was adamant that he would build the wall, just as he promised during his campaign. So he told Congressional leaders they should use the money and include it in the 2017 spending bill to fund the project which is expected to cost up to 15 billion dollars and possibly more. Trump's plan was to extract the money from Mexico during his future negotiations over NAFTA.

"There's no way that's going to happen. It's not a matter of how much does it cost...it's a matter of dignity and national sovereignty."
— Luis Videgaray Caso

But Mexico's President Peña Nieto lays out his terms and they are not in agreement with Trump. Nieto pledged to fight for Mexico's interests in upcoming talks with Trump. The Mexican leader vowed not to back down and unveiled a list of 10 goals. Mexico gave a commitment to preserve tariff-free commerce under NAFTA although Trump has said he would renegotiate. Also, they want the continued free-flow of remittances from Mexican nationals in the U.S. to their family members back home. The remittances are worth about 25 billion dollars; it's the money Trump plans to seize and use to pay for "the wall" he is using U.S. money to build along the Mexican border.

"We are prepared to quit NAFTA if we are offered a bad deal, there may be no other option."
— Ildefonso Guajardo
Mexico's Economic Minister

Threat or Not

Trump didn't stop there, and no one ever thought he would. Trump never stops until he gets what he wants. In January 24, 2017, Trump signed an Executive Order suspending refugee resettlement for 120 days and barring it indefinitely for Syria. The Order didn't stop there. It barred other immigrants, including professionals and green card holders from seven majority Muslim countries.

"The goal is to keep out radical Islamic terrorists."
— Trump

Since instituting rigorous refugee screening in 1980, the U.S. has given sanctuary to over three million people, all fleeing from religious, racial or political persecution. Since then, the country hasn't been attacked by terrorists from any of them. Therefore, other than Trump, few believe they are a threat. The odds of a U.S. citizen being killed from a terrorist attack by a refugee on American soil are infinitesimal; actually more like 1 in 3.6 billion, according to the Cato Institute. It is the home-grown terrorists that are the immediate threat to the U.S.

"We want to ensure that we are not
admitting into our country
the very threats our soldiers are fighting overseas."
— *Trump*

It didn't take long for the people to react; the backlash was swift. On January 28th, massive protests erupted at airports nationwide. Without hesitation, the ACLU and other rights groups quickly took action. They filed lawsuits that would halt deportations under the Order. They took legal action in at least four states. Then another major disruption occurred when acting Attorney General, Sally Yates from the former Obama Administration, expressed to federal prosecutors not to defend the Order. She stated she wasn't sure that the Order from Trump was on point with the Justice Department. She believed that she should always seek justice and stand for what is right. But it did not help her career within the Trump Administration.

"YOU"RE FIRED!"
— *Trump*

Those were the only words she heard. Afterwards, Trump said that increased vetting of immigrants and refugees was needed and had been undertaken by Democrats under Obama. Trump's lawyers believed the courts would have a hard time proving that the Order targets Muslims. But they were wrong.

"In instant outrage, Iraq voted to bar Americans entry. Britain's House of Commons unanimously condemned the Order and protests continued in the U.S. But for Trump, outrage may have been the point."

No White House

The New England Patriots did it again. They became the 2017 Super Bowl Champs. The party began with Tom Brady and Donald Trump. They are friends and Donald is a fan of the New England Patriots. But the champagne hadn't been completely poured before Martellus Bennett, the New England Patriot's tight end, overshadowed the celebration when he refused to attend the NFL team's victory photo-op at the White House with Trump.

"There's no way!"
— Martellus Bennett

After Bennett stated his case about how he felt about Trump's feelings for blacks, he told the team there's no way he was attending the event.

"I don't feel welcome in that house. I'll leave it at that."
— *LeGarrette Blount*

He made it clear to anybody who was listening. After his announcement, five more of Bennett's teammates stated they felt the same way and decided to join the boycott with Bennett. What is so ironic is that the Patriot's is considered "Trump's Team." The President is a friend of Tom Brady, Coach Belichick and the team's owner, Robert Kraft. It is understandable why team members who are black would boycott. Trump has routinely portrayed black America as riddled with crime and poverty. He also made the drastic decision to appoint Steve Bannon, a white supremacist as his strategic advisor. It's obvious that Trump is not on the same page with blacks and doesn't have respect for them.

"If it ain't white it ain't right."

This is how Trump views people in his world and the world he controls.

> *"Some athletes can't stomach*
> *the thought of shaking his hand."*
> — *Roy S. Johnson*

Chapter Thirty-nine

EU Worried

The European Council President Donald Tusk believes U.S. President Donald Trump is a threat to European security. He feels that Trump is just as big a threat as Russia and Islamist terrorism.

> *"The change in Washington puts the European Union in a difficult situation with the new Administration seeming to put into question the last 70 years of American Foreign Policy."*
> — *Donald Tusk*

He stated the above comment in a letter to EU (European Union) member states. European leaders have expressed dismay at Trump's support for the UK's decision to leave the Bloc, and they fear his support of NATO, the main guarantor of

European security, is tepid. Trump has criticized rules set by the EU—which he called "THE CONSORTIUM"—for hampering construction work at his Irish golf course. All of that had Tusk worried.

Rule Breaker

It has been two years and Donald Trump has made a living out of mastering the art of discomposure. If it was a political principle, he disregarded it or disrespected it while he disrupted his way to the White House. But disruption in government, Mr. do-it-his-way-or-nothing, the rule maker who breaks what seems like all the rules, had possibly bitten off more than he could chew. In the first three months of his Presidency, the billionaire real estate mogul has witnessed the cost of being at the helm of America. Four federal judges have frozen his hastily issued Executive Order banning immigrants from specific countries from entering the United States.

Intelligence officials have leaked descriptions of classified intercepts that forced Trump to fire Michael Flynn, his National Security Advisor. Evidently it was reported that Michael Flynn had misled the nation about his ties with a Russian diplomat. Then there were more leaks, according to the "New York Times" that came from current and former officials that claimed Trump campaign aides and senior Russian intelligence officials had actually been in contact during the 2016 Presidential campaign. Trump was pushed to retreat from his pledge in December 2016 to provide more recognition to the government in Taiwan by the President of China, Xi Jinping.

Protesters began interrupting normal business, town hall meetings by lawmakers in front of Trump Towers, airports and through the streets of the U.S. while Republicans are wondering did they make the right choice. They were growing restless with the disruptions of Trump; with the White House Oversight Committee probing Trump's security protocol after he discussed classified information during a weekend retreat at his estate in Mar-a-lago; the Majority Senate Leader announced that the Senate investigation of Russian interference in the U.S. election would expand; Trump accused former President Obama of wiretapping him without providing any evidence; and White House Press Secretary Sean Spicer apologized for U.K. surveillance claim when he said Obama used British intelligence to spy on Trump. Others in the GOP have raised concerns that their legislative hopes under the Unified Republicans will fade after all the misunderstandings over Trump's priorities on issues such as tax reform and trade.

"There are a lot of questions on the part of the people who took the President home after the dance."
— *Senator Pat Roberts*

The White House was in such a state of confusion with so many Trump distractions that his staff and Administration was having a hard time working on things which mattered. Trump as President was like watching a reality show with his rants and excessive Tweeting. There was internecine drama between senior aides who spent their days mixing government business while jockeying for position in efforts to impress the billionaire President. The White House Chief of Staff, Reince Priebus, was truly feeling the pressure more than anyone who had been appointed the head man in charge by the rule breaker. He continually found himself rushing down the hallway from his office to intercept visitors to the Oval Office who were not on the President's schedule. It's hard to be in charge when snipers are following the

President in efforts to assassinate him. Running the White House everyday on a normal basis can be overwhelming. But to run it for Donald Trump is overpowering.

"Very little takes place in the White House without complication or contradiction."

His Administration is forced into positions to constantly have to defend the moves of Trump through the media, TV and press conferences. Even Kellyanne Conway, who had been quick to boast she has direct access to Trump, stated to the world that Flynn had the full confidence of Trump. And what has become the norm:

"The cleanup man is sent in with an attempt to try and correct it. Trump appears to have to be cleaned up afterwards a lot."

Likely Guilty

After being forced to resign, Michael Flynn stated he would testify but only if the courts would grant him immunity. It's kind of confusing why he would ask for immunity unless he believed or knew that he was committing a crime. In 2016 when Hillary asked for immunity, Flynn and Trump both declared that only people guilty of a crime would need immunity. And yet, less than a year later, Michael Flynn finds himself in the same position as Hillary. But the huge question that is on everybody's mind is:

"Does Flynn have any valid, incriminating evidence against Trump?

Is Trump trembling in his shoes? Will Michael Flynn be the one to bring down Trump? The world is waiting to see, although the Trump Administration said that Flynn should testify. The world wonders if Flynn has the goods on Trump and why does he really want immunity? But his testimony would turn out to not hurt Trump who proved to be untouchable.

"Is it good information or is it good lawyering?"
— "CNN"

Trump once said about Hillary, "If you need immunity, you're likely guilty of a crime."

Cahoots

It is my belief that Trump is in cahoots with the Russians. This is the reason why he strongly feels it is important to get along with Russia. It has been revealed that Trump had several talks about having Trump buildings built in Russia during his run for the Presidency. And it has been reported that he made more promises to President Putin that if he did win the Presidency he would lift sanctions that would allow Russia to drill in the ocean for oil which is worth trillions of dollars. That is why there is so much suspicion that Russia interfered with the U.S. election. They had good reason to do so. It was to their advantage for Hillary to lose because she would not play their game. Therefore, they hacked into her email account to create the email scandal. They wanted her to look like a liar when the true liar was always Donald J. Trump. He was and has always been a liar and a fraud.

But you may ask if this is true why hasn't Trump lifted the sanctions on Russia? It's because he's not trustworthy. He's the king of lies. He's probably backed out of the Agreement or he just hasn't done it yet. There's too much heat on him right now with the Russia investigation in progress.

Plus, he'd already gotten what he wanted and that's all that mattered. You are what you are and the truth always reveals itself.

Chapter Forty

Assad Must Go

The President was faced with another challenge in his first 100 days and it was a challenge he could not ignore. It was reported that on April 4, 2017, there was another attack on Syria. But unlike other attacks it was a chemical attack which murdered 92 people, including children. The President's first reaction was to point the finger at former President Obama and his Administration. It was a sad sight to see on "CNN" as they showed children who had suffered from the chemical attack. They were being hosed down with water and fighting to breathe as the fought to survive the horrific attack. The people demanded that Trump do something. Trump replied, "I'm not the President of the world, I'm President of the United States." But U.S. Ambassador Nikki Haley stated clearly:

"If you don't act on the Syria attack, we will!"
— *U.S. Ambassador Nikki Haley*

She stated that the heinous actions by President Assad can't be tolerated which forced President Trump to step up.

"It is my responsibility to respond to the Syrian attack. We have a big problem. We have somebody who is not doing the right thing."
— *President Trump*

He said the world is a mess and that as President he inherited a mess but vowed the U.S> would fix it. His Administration acknowledged the Syrian attack and called it an "affront to humanity." They were loudly calling out the President of Syria. Trump replied he would respond to the attack but wouldn't say how. He didn't want Assad to know what his next move would be.

"ASSAD MUST GO!"
— *Bill Richardson*

The President stated that the attack on the children made a huge impact on him and he called the attack a "Horrible, horrible thing," and that it changed his mind about just being the President of the United States.

"Assad, Russia and Iran have no interest in peace."
— U.S. Ambassador Nikki Haley

Ambassador Haley blasted Russia over the Syria attack but Trump uses softer words and the world can only wait to see what Trump will do.

"Before Trump was the President he talked tough. But now that Syria has brought the fight to him, he doesn't talk tough, said nothing about Russia, and only blames the former President."
— Patterson

Assad Regime

President Bashar Al-Assad is a vicious man with an equally vicious extermination policy. Under his command the Syrian regime has executed over 13,000 people over a six-year span of civil war. He has implemented mass hangings north of

Damascus that was rumored to be nicknamed "the slaughter house." Based on a damning report from people who were incarcerated at Saydnaya Prison and interviews from former guards, judges and Amnesty International that on a weekly basis, since the start of 2011to 2015, prison officials extracted numerous prisoners from their cells and beat them lifeless or hanged them in the middle of the night or murdered them in secrecy. Assad would also target civilian activists who opposed the President. Thousands more inmates were tortured, starved to death or died from lack of water. Although the Assad regime stated that the report was false, it was evident that thousands of people had disappeared, turned up dead or was never released alive after being thrown into that prison.

> "He has to be stopped!" The question is:
> can President Donald J. Trump do it?"
>
> — Mr. Genaro

Years of previous attempts to stop Assad or change his behavior has failed. There were 92 people killed in the chemical attack and 32 of them were children.

Retaliation

President Trump played the trump card. He didn't talk tough and instead retaliated swiftly and deadly. Without hesitation, Trump launched military strikes against Syria. But before launching 69 Tomahawk missiles, the U.S. notified Russia's military that they were going to strike Syria's airbase in retaliation of Syria violating its treaty obligations under the Chemical Weapons Convention. The U.S. felt it was their duty to notify Russia using the "Deconfliction Hotline" ahead of the Syrian strike. Trump believed that Assad had gone too far and needed to feel the wrath of the U.S. It was his intention to send a clear message that chemical weapons, bloodshed and slaughter would not be tolerated.

"Trump calls for civilized nations to help end slaughter and bloodshed in Syria."
— *President Trump*

The Pentagon's initial approach was to strike severely to damage or destroy Syrian aircraft and Syrian state TV.

"This is an act of aggression that leads to losses."
— *Pentagon*

Russia warns the U.S. of negative consequences but was not clear about what was meant. The U.S. believed that Russia would stand on the sideline and let Syria accept its punishment, but the world would have to wait and see. The U.S. had gotten fed up with Assad who had killed thousands and thousands of children, men and women with bombs.

"Assad choked out the lives of children, helpless women, babies and men who had been murdered in barbaric ways."
— *United States*

And Trump ordered missiles fired from the USS Porter and USS Ross naval ships. Now the world waited to see:

"What happens next?"

The Syrian opposition commander hoped the U.S. strike would be a turning point in the six-year war. But the next move is on Syria. Russia's President Putin stated,

"The U.S. act of aggression was a violation of international law."
— *President Putin*

But President Trump stated no child of God should ever have to suffer a slow and terrible death as he made the decision—48 hours after the chemical strike and without Congress approval—to strike Syria's air base where chemical weapons were stored.

"Trump separated himself from former President Obama and showed he had balls and used his authority to let the world know he was not afraid to attack or afraid of a war."
— *Patterson*

Six were killed in the attack.

American   Money   Publishing

WE PUBLISH THE REALIST BOOKS

Chapter Forty-one

Having Dinner

Donald Trump had his pedal to the metal. He had let Syria and Russia know he was not one to be played with. He fired off 59 missiles from the naval destroyer USS Porter and the missile destroyer USS Ross in the deep waters of the ocean in the middle of the darkness. Bombs flew through the night at 500 miles per hour. It took approximately one hour to reach and hit Syria's air base where Trump believed Syria stored chemical weapons. But what was so cold and detached about the attack...

> *"Trump was having dinner with the President of China while it was all taking place."*
> — *Patterson*

A Governor said the airstrike caused the death of six people but there are always casualties of war. Trump's ultimate intention was to send Assad a message that chemical warfare would not be tolerated. Not then or ever as long as America was in power.

President Trump inherited several undeclared wars when he took office. He started off overseeing several ongoing combat operations that started with Bush and lingered on into the Obama Administration.   One is the 8,400 U.S. troops deployed in Afghanistan, the longest running war ever in U.S. history. They were there to train, assist and prepare Afghanistan troops for their fight against the Taliban.   There were another 5,000 troops assisting the Iraqi army who was fighting head-to-head with ISIS. And still another 500 U.S. Special Forces fighters who were leading the battle against ISIS in Syria. And in Yemen, the United States was targeting Al Qaida in the Arab Peninsula and helping Saudi Arabia fight a proxy war against Iranian-backed rebels. The wars were so hectic that a day before Trump's Inauguration the Pentagon sent two B-2 bombers to take out suspected ISIS camps in Libya. In addition to those strikes, the United States have bases scattered all around the globe in places like Turkey, South Korea, Japan, Saudi Arabia, Spain, Germany and Djibouti. But Trump took the battles head-on, including Syria with Assad at the helm after the chemical attacks. A few countries around the world, like Israel, displayed their disappointment. But Trump didn't care. He talked tough and he backed it up.

"Nuff said. Put up or shut up."
— *Patterson*

Full of Problems

It was starting to look like the Trump Administration was beginning to take shape. Trump's first American policy was beginning to look more like a sort of "realpolitik" where moral considerations were shed in favor of accomplishing transactional "wins" on jobs and security. Although he promotes America first he doesn't act as if American's are squeaky clean. He is more drawn to autocrats and cynical and is cynical about promoting cherished American ideals. When Trump was asked about the violent reputation of Russian President Putin who had ordered political killings, Trump spoke without hesitation.

"Do you think our country is so innocent?"
— Trump

His Administration has lifted human rights conditions on the sale of F-16 fighters to Bahrain where they have political nonconformist incarcerated without giving them due process. Trump also spewed about Egyptian strongman Abdel Fattah al-Sisi who savagely cracked down on political nonconformists. But no matter the power of America and Trump, America can't and won't be able to right every wrong. There is no secret that human rights matter. No matter what religion or race you are—or choose to be on this planet—if you suffer because of any type of persecution or is singled out in any way for any perceived "difference" or must endure human-imposed suffering on a mass scale, it will not be tolerated in 2017. Yet, there are still human rights renegades such as North Korea, described as a prison parading country that utilized active gulags and forced their people into starvation. There are civil wars where people are being gassed o death. People are living in horrific circumstances where their main focus is to try to stay alive. Where fair human rights is only a dream, gasping for air to breathe, still in 2017. Could Donald Trump change that? Or better yet, does he want to?

"I am not the President of the world. I am the President of the United States. It's America first."
— *Donald J. Trump*

What was the most powerful man in the world to do in a world with unlimited pain; a world that suffered from inhumanity where the U.S. and Trump were not interested in global government or police to ride to the rescue? And to make matters worse, what was Trump to do when nations like China and Egypt—countries that were in Washington's vital national interest to maintain a business relationship—but they still committed acts which pulled at anyone's moral boundary while completely disregarding any notion of human rights. Although America is the most powerful country in the world, it still has limits in its ability to control global events. Just because Trump controls a military that is second to none, it does not mean he has the power to fix everything that goes wrong nor can he solve every problem.

The world is full of problems created by other governments or dictators. Plus, when Trump makes a decision to fix a problem, he banks on other countries turning against America and becomes an ally of the enemy. For example, if Trump clamps down on Egypt for human rights violations or break off relations, Egypt could take its revenge on Israel or decide to join forces with Iran, just as Trump suggested to China to put North Korea in check about their testing of nuclear weapons. If China doesn't calm down North Korea and the U.S. steps in, it could cause the U.S. and China to sever relations. It would be a recipe for disaster with all the trade and human rights issues that could lead to war. President Trump reacted to Syria after a chemical attack on their people which ignited a strong reaction from Russia.

> *"The U.S. military attack was on*
> *the brink of military clash."*
>
> — *Russia*

Putin's next move is of major concern for Trump and America. Russia says the U.S. is one step away from military action. But Russia has been either complicit or simply incompetent said Nikki Haley.

"We are prepared to do more.
But we hope that is not necessary."
— *U.S. Ambassador Nikki Haley*

Fired

Trump would shock the world again and without warning he fired FBI Director James Comey. It seemed to come out of nowhere but when it came, it was swift and surprising. The firing occurred in May 2017 and the people wondered if it was a cover-up. Comey was investigating possible ties between the Trump campaign and Russia, although Trump stated in an interview that Director Comey told him he was not under investigation.

"I believe the President is obstructing justice."
— *Senator Tim Kaine*

But Trump said it had nothing to do with Russia and everything to do with confidence. He said Comey lost the confidence of almost everyone in Washington, including Republicans and Democrats.

But others believed that he was one of the most dominating figures since J. Edgar Hoover. At first, it was reported that Comey was fired for using the word concealed in his speech concerning the investigation of Hillary Clinton.

"I would do it again. I could go public or I could have concealed it."

— FBI Comey

But the Trump Administration claims the FBI is never supposed to consider concealing any type of evidence and should never have been spoken out of the mouth of a FBI Director. Trump stated Comey was fired to restore public trust and confidence in the agency. Trump believed Comey mishandled the Clinton email investigation.

"You are not able to effectively lead the bureau."

— Trump

Comey first learned he was fired while giving a presentation offsite and the attendees saw the news flash on a TV monitor mounted behind Comey and brought it to his attention. Senator Burr said he was troubled by the timing. It stank like a cover-up.

But Trump is eccentric and very unpredictable. Therefore, nothing should surprise anyone anymore.

> *"It's like Trump is still on his reality show.*
> *He is constantly firing people."*
> — *Patterson*

> *"The Trump Administration chose to defame*
> *me, and more importantly, the FBI."*
> — *James Comey*

But after the former FBI Director's testimony, Comey did not provide enough evidence to prove obstruction of justice charges. But he did testify that Trump is a liar.

American　　　　Money　　　Publishing

WE PUBLISH THE REALIST BOOKS

Chapter Forty-two

North Korea Threat

Kim Jong Un decided he didn't care what Trump or the United States were saying. They had given him several warnings to stop testing and firing off his missiles but it was to no avail. Trump urged China to interfere but China remained silent. Despite the warnings, Kim Jong Un fired off another missile that was estimated could have reached Hawaii, Guam or San Diego if it had been fired horizontally instead of vertically. North Korea also created a nuclear war head small enough to fit on the head of a missile. It was reported that North Korea's missiles could reach the territory of Guam in only 14 minutes, making them an immediate threat to the United States. Kim Jong Un has proven to be more successful than his father with his ability to create a stronger and larger military to threaten America.

The blame has been placed on Bill Clinton. The former President made a bad deal with North Korea, giving to the country four billion dollars while allowing them to secretly build threatening missiles and nuclear warheads. After several threats and with the testing of a missile in July 2017, Trump decided to place sanctions on North Korea which would cost them a billion dollars a year. Kim Jong Un was furious. "America will pay for this!" he fumed and Trump responded immediately. "Any North Korean threat will be met with "fire and fury." The world was put on edge as Trump continued. "Kim Jong Un better not make any more threats." Donald J. Trump, the President of the United States, refused to back down. Why would he? He was the new Hitler who secretly didn't care about war but possibly wanted it to allow him the opportunity to wipe out the Koreans. North Korea called Trump's warning "a load of nonsense." Kim Jong Un then threatened to fire off four ballistic missiles and to attack Guam—a mainland on U.S. soil—with a strategic nuclear attack. Trump tells the U.S., "That's why the first thing I did was strengthen our military because there will never be a time that we are not the most powerful military in the world. Nobody is going to threaten us with anything."

But North Korea refuses to back down as Kim Jong Un and Trump argue back and forth. Kim vows to mercilessly wipe out the provocateurs. Trump refused to negotiate although it was a huge threat to destroy a regime and their people with the power the U.S. holds, according to General Mattis. He told the world that maybe his threat wasn't tough enough. When asked by reporters what he meant by that, he responded, "You'll see." The last time he said "you'll see" he fired missiles without any warning. But the world didn't have long to wait to find out what he meant because the next morning he Tweeted, "The U.S. military is 'locked and loaded' and aimed at North Korea," boasting about the U.S. military and how serious he was about war.

Russia and China would finally weigh in on the threat and would make an attempt to prevent North Korea and a U.S. conflict. China tells the world if North Korea fires the first missile, China would stand down. But if the U.S. fires first, China would align with North Korea and Kim Jong Un. China is North Korea's closest and strongest ally and maybe that's what Kim Jong Un was banking on. There was talk about whether Kim Jong Un was suicidal? Did he have no regard for life? The same was speculated about Donald Trump but it was obvious, just like with Hitler, millions of people would die under the leadership of Trump. Because of his boasting, it was reported that it was proof that the U.S. is really the master threat to a nuclear war because Trump refused to back down or negotiate. Trump responded, "I would like to de-nuke the world," but goes on to say, "see what happens if he fires anything at Guam."

North Korea began to feel like Trump was forcing their hand and calling their bluff. "Trump is driving the U.S. toward the brink of nuclear war." Mattis warns, "A war would be catastrophic and if he doesn't realize the need to negotiate, the U.S. has the power to destroy the regime and the people." Guam began to make preparation for a potential attack by Kim Jong Un as well as Hawaii who began to practice drills. In the past, North Korea has been known to change their behavior when China steps in and becomes serious.   The former Commanding Officer of the guided-missile destroyer USS Cole, Commander Kirk Lippold, USN (Retired), stated, "We need to prepare to shoot the missile down." President Trump went on TV after boycotting reporters for the first eight months of his term and said, "If he does anything in respect to Guam or anywhere on American territory, he will regret it and regret it fast." The "Guam Pacific Daily" newspaper had "14 Minutes" on its front page, letting the people know that's how long it would take for the missile to reach and strike Guam.

No American President had ever spoken in the way Trump had as he continued to talk tough and not back down from Kim Jong Un who stated he is examining the operational planning to strike areas around Guam. Even if America doesn't go to war with North Korea, there is still no doubt that millions will die under the leadership of Trump. But as of now, his bold threats makes North Korea back down. "Donald Trump is a gangster and mentally deranged. He will pay dearly and face consequences beyond his expectations," Kim Jong Un stated. But Trump showed no fear as he responded with, "North Korean leaders won't be around much longer if they strike the U.S." A North Korean top diplomat said, "A strike against the U.S. is inevitable which would obviously be a declaration of war."

Before Trump's four years as President are up North Korea will probably have become a nuclear country. It appears they've reached the road of no return. They have flagrantly violated international law and it will get worse. North Korea doesn't care about sanctions and they're not worried about what China or the United States might do. They have repeatedly stated they will not stop or turn back their weapons program because they feel it is the best decision for their future. Both China and Russia have nuclear weapons. North Korea feels they should have them, too. They have backed the U.S. and Donald Trump into a corner and it's time for the end game. North Korea feels as if they're a full-fledged nuclear power.

On September 1st it was reported there was a 6.3 magnitude tremor detected. It turned out it was actually Kim Jong Un successfully testing his new hydrogen bomb. They have boasted that they have nuclear warheads and aren't afraid to use them. North Korea has become the most dangerous place on the planet by performing their most powerful nuclear tests ever. Kim Jong Un is crazy, unstable and dead serious. He wants to be able to come to the table as one of the heads of the world. From the stance he has taken, there are only two choices: Either annihilate him and his country, or allow him to become an accepted nuclear country. The next move is on Trump. What will the tough talking

President do? I believe he will tuck his tail and cower, but maybe not. What we do know is North Korea has stated they will do no negotiation. It's as if Kim Jong Un is begging for war, clearly stating either put up or shut up.

"Look in the mirror...
White America voted you in."
— David Duke

Chapter Forty-three

Neo-Nazi/KKK/White Supremacist and Trump

"I think Donald Trump is a white supremacist and chief."
— *Bakari Sellers (D)*
Former South Carolina
House Member

UNFIT TO SERVE!

On August 12, 2017, during a violent protest at a white nationalist rally in Charlottesville, Virginia, a strike was made at American law and justice where one person was killed and many injured. Trump failed to condemn the Ku Klux Klan,

Neo-Nazis and white supremacists after one of their people purposely drove his car into a crowd and ran over a 32-year old counter-protester named Heather Heyer, killing her. The media blasted Trump for making it appear as if the counter-protesters were just as much at fault as the white supremacist groups. Governor Terry McAuliffe (D) of Virginia clearly stated, "KKK, Neo-Nazi and white supremacist extremist groups I have a clear message for you...Go home! There is no place for you here in Virginia. We don't want you here. Leave! Go home and don't come back."

As President of the United States Trump did not and would not call the evildoers by name, although he's never held his tongue when calling others thugs, rapists, drug dealers, liars, radical Islamic terrorists, etc. David Duke, the leader of the Ku Klux Klan, Tweeted, "Don't forget who voted you into your position." Trump made no response but why would he? It's obvious that white nationalists felt he could possibly be one of them. They are his biggest supporters and it's under his leadership he has made America hate again. Just like Hitler, the Nazis are obviously his people. They love him, respect him and voted for him. He is their chosen President. So after three days of being pressured the President finally called out the KKK, Neo-Nazis and white supremacist extremist groups. It was something the President did not want to do. He found himself in a Catch-22; he was "damned if he do and damned if he don't." But finally he put the country first. However, the people felt he "was a day late and a dollar short" and "too little too late." In his next press conference, he would express how he truly felt. "White supremacists were not the only ones violent. There were very fine people on both sides and you had a group on the other side that was very bad and I'm not afraid to say it," he said as he stood up for the people who killed Heather Heyer.

Apparently, Trump tolerates bigotry. He makes excuses for the white supremacists as he blames both sides for the Charlottesville violence. David Duke Tweeted, "Look in the mirror. White America voted you in." When Trump didn't speak against David Duke and the KKK, it made them feel they had a President who accepted them. Then David Duke accepted him for his courageous speech when he blamed the counter-protesters. Republicans, Democrats and the people were finally starting to see Trump for who he really was. "They weren't all white nationalists. The group other than

Neo-Nazis and white nationalists were violent, too." It took eight months as the U.S. President for Trump to start showing the world his true colors. Trump was actually the new Hitler. And he wasn't afraid to show it.

> *"Trump defends Charlottesville Nazis"*
> — *White Supremacist*

It is believed that his reason for being so adamant in defending Neo-Nazis, the KKK and extremist groups is motivated by his Chief Strategist, Steve Bannon, who is a master manipulator of Trump. But Trump doesn't like anyone thinking someone controls or manipulates him which is why he blurts out his famous phrase so often: "You're fired!" Less than eight months in office, Bannon was out. The architect of the strategy which got Trump elected was finally out.

> *"I may be out but I won't be silenced. The Trump Presidency which we fought for and won is over. Now I'm free. I've got my hands back on my weapons. I am definitely going to crush the opposition."*
> — *Steve Bannon*

*"Trump amplified bigotry and it is likely he
will never recover as the U.S. President."*
— *Mr. Genaro*

*"BEFORE IT'S ALL SAID AND DONE, JUST LIKE WITH
HITLER, MILLIONS WILL DIE UNDER THE LEADERSHIP
OF TRUMP"*

Trump has been the President of the United States for over a year and in that time he has revealed many things about himself. He obviously wanted to reverse everything Obama had accomplished, regardless if it was good for the country or not. The media, CNN, ET and TMZ all exposed signs of the President having mental issues. Democrats attempted to get Trump on "obstruction of justice" charges. But it was only after ex-National Security Advisor Michael Flynn was charged with making false statements to the FBI that we saw events pointing to the beginning of the end for Trump. "The President cannot obstruct justice," his lawyer stated. And Trump graciously continued to run the country. But rumors throughout the halls of the White House whispered that the White House was being powered by a dysfunctional man. The White House was in chaos. Trump had no clue what he was doing. Democrats challenged whether he was mentally challenged and unfit to be the American President.

Fire and Fury, a new book by Michael Wolff, would reveal hidden secrets related to the President's mental capacity. "He's impulsive and volatile," a psychiatrist stated, "and he's unraveling. He's actually losing a grip on reality." The book suggests he's paranoid; that his daughter Ivanka is a dumb blond; and Trump is delusional and bipolar. Democrats (56 of them) have backed a bill for the panel to remove him from office. His erratic behavior has many politicians questioning his ability to lead the country. They point out his flaws with the direct order to impeach him: "The President is not above the law." And his son, Donald Trump, Jr. is being questioned about his part in the Russia investigation while they're investigating Trump who is on a Twitter rampage with Kim Jong Un, making enemies daily. Trump doesn't believe in one war at a time. He believes the more enemies the more honor as if he isn't the U.S. President but more of a dictator. He fired his good friend, Steve Bannon then said he lost his mind, but only after Bannon opened up behind the scene secrets of Trump's behavior. They couldn't figure out his thought process. He called the continent of Africa stupid, displaying his hate and his stupidity. He refused to apologize and his actions confused everybody; nothing like an ordinary man. But Trump is not like the ordinary, he is extraordinary and the world is being introduced to Hitler reborn again.

Epilogue

Trump: the New Hitler

"The Germans and the Austrians would never make a comparison to Adolf Hitler lightly."
— *Gerfried Sperl*

It is becoming very noticeable that foreigners are finding parallels between the 2016 new President Trump and the Hitler of the early 1930's before the Nazi leader set in motion the machinery for mass murder.

"Like Hitler, Trump is extraordinarily talented at manipulating the press. And also like him, hold truth to be entirely irrelevant."
— *Timothy Snyder*
American History

Of course it is not truly believed that Trump is not THE NEW HITLER. But he did speak on the edge of national ideas in his Inaugural address. His speech was a religiously-charged battle prayer which neither Democracy nor human rights were mentioned. What Trump actually did was pay homage to patriotism, which was to be defended with blood. With his selection of Steve Bannon as his Chief Strategist, perhaps that part of the speech was written by Bannon. It was rumored that Bannon had been pulling all the strings someone told the "Hollywood Reporter." "Trump's term would be as exciting as the 1930's and usher in an economic nationalist movement." Any man or woman who knows the history of Hitler, upon hearing those words, could only think of the Nazi era. It was no secret that Trump's inaugural address sounded,

"Remarkably similar to Hitler's first address as a German Chancellor in 1933."
— Boris Reitschuster

The address was also viewed by Igor Eidman, a Russian sociologist, as Trump hitting the same themes as Hitler: first describing the country as a horror-scape of poverty and violence; blaming the crisis on selfish, sellout leaders; and finally promising that henceforth "the people" alone would rule. Obviously it would be "irresponsible and stupid" to conclude from his speech that Trump will follow Hitler's path.

> "But it would be just as irresponsible not to notice the similarities and heed the lessons."

— Boris Reitschuster

DONALD J. TRUMP IS THE NEW HITLER...

Please leave a review on Amazon.com

Coming Soon…

(An Excerpt)

AMERICAN
MONEY
PUBLISHING

DYLANN ROOF

Evil, Pure Evil in White America

Written By
Genaro Patterson

American   Money   Publishing

WE PUBLISH THE REALIST BOOKS

Prologue

Pure Evil

He walked in as if he was seeking the spirit of the Lord God Almighty after he entered the Emanuel African Methodist Episcopal (AME) Church in Charleston, South Carolina. Bible study was in session and the people inside the black church accepted him as if he was one of them, even though he had pure white skin, blue eyes and blond hair. But to the black folks of that church, they didn't see color. All they saw was the Lord. They had no clue that when they would close their eyes to pray to God Almighty, the young man they had allowed into their church was a white supremacist and would try to kill them all because of the hatred he had instilled in his heart. He would wait patiently until Bible study was over and they closed their eyes to pray because he wanted them to know their God could not save them once he released his wrath of hate that would come from the fatal bullets from his gun he had brought into the church with him. He had a .45 automatic and would begin shooting a constant stream of gunfire, targeting everything that was black.

With their eyes closed and saying the words they believed God wanted to hear, the prayer was interrupted by rapid gunfire. BLADA! BLADA! BLADA! BLADA! BLADA! BLADA! The gunfire seemed never ending as people fell to the ground from fatal gunshot wounds. Someone screamed in panic, "He has a gun!" Tywanza Sanders yelled to alert everyone. Even as he yelled the warning, Rev. Clementa Pinckney was being gunned down. Pinckney was the 41-year old Pastor of Emanuel AME Church and a State Senator for South Carolina. Panic, chaos and pandemonium quickly kicked in. BLADA! BLADA! BLADA! BLADA! BLADA! The gunfire continued and Felicia Sanders' son was hit BLADA! BLADA! The bullets had no names and their targets were the color black. Tywanza was instantly hit because once he heard the shots, he opened his eyes and heard the shouts of his mother and launched forward in an attempt to stop the evil man who was slaughtering people in a church where they went to worship a God they believed in. But the 26-year old had no chance against the Glock .45 caliber pistol that kept firing.

Dylann Roof was evil. He wanted to kill everyone in the building and then leave to do the same thing in other buildings where blacks congregated. He had more addresses in his car. He was on some kind of kill-all-the-blacks-and-anyone-who-supported-them type movement. His plan was calculated and concocted against black people. Women and children ran and hid under tables, hoping their God would save them, but people were constantly being shot down. BLADA! BLADA! BLADA! BLADA! The bullets were tearing through the flesh of prominent men and women. The harmless looking white boy proved to be evil as he relentlessly pulled the trigger on the Glock .45 over 70 times, hitting his targets more than 60 times.

> *"But many more Dylann Roof's*
> *remain, waiting to strike again.*
> *The only question is, when?"*
> — *Mr. Genaro*

33 Federal Counts

Dylann Storm Roof was facing the federal death penalty. He was accused of the massacre which took place in a South Carolina church where nine lives were taken. His day in court was extremely emotional as the jury heard heart-wrenching testimony from those who were fortunate enough to survive the brutal attack that left nine dead. On the opening day of the much publicized trial there was testimony from both the Federal Bureau of Investigation (FBI) agents and South and North Carolina law enforcement. It was December 7, 2016; the day the world would finally get a chance to see why Dylann Roof was so mad and so evil. They would finally hear the details of the brutal and unsavory manner in which the June 17, 2015 killings were carried out. Hopefully, they would find out why the white supremacist vowed to murder black, defenseless people. The trial would show in detail jurors, lawyers and courtroom observers crying with faces wet from tears.

You could hear a pin drop as survivor Felicia Sanders (age 58) gave her testimony on the witness stand. The testimony would impact several people as local television reporters videotaped and took notes on the entire trial. Dylann Roof was finally on trial and he was charged with 33 federal counts which included hate crimes for the shooting of nine black parishioners during a Bible study at Emanuel AME Church. Felicia testified that Dylann Roof did not start shooting until after the Bible study class was complete and everyone stood up, closed their eyes and began to pray. She said after she closed her eyes and was talking to God, she heard a loud bang and opened her eyes. What she saw was the visitor they had allowed to join their study and had allowed into their sanctuary had a gun in his hand. She was instantly horrified and screamed out, "He has a gun!" She said she yelled out to alert everyone but by then Dylann Roof had already shot 41-year old Rev. Clementa Pinckney, the pastor of the church and a State Senator for South Carolina.

She also witnessed the shooting and killing of her own son, 26-year old Tywanza, who was killed making an effort to try to stop the white supremacist.

"I watched my son come into the world,
and I watched my son leave this world."
— *Felicia Sanders*

She couldn't hold her composure and became so distraught that U.S. District Judge Richard Gergel made a heartfelt decision to call for a recess. And after the recess, Felicia Sanders came back to continue her testimony. She told jurors about being terrified and her terror when she attempted to shelter her granddaughter—who fortunately survived because of her heroic act. She hid her underneath a table while witnessing her son and her 87-year old aunt, Susie Jackson, being gunned down with seemingly no remorse. She testified that Dylann Roof had a blank expression on his face which matched the indifference of his demeanor; the same demeanor on display as he sat at the defense table. Dylann Roof didn't care. He never looked up and had already told the world:

> *"I AM NOT SORRY"*
> *— Dylann Storm Roof*

At one point, Attorney David Bruck, the attorney who represented the heartless, evil Dylann Roof, moved for the judge to declare a mistrial after Felicia's testimony. He told the court she testified to what Roof's sentence should be in front of the jury. He said it was inappropriate. But the judge quickly dismissed it. He was not about to let such an evil person get off the hook so easy. During cross-examination, Attorney Bruck asked Ms. Sanders if she recalled Mr. Roof saying anything after the shootings. She replied:

"He said he was going to kill himself," she said. "I was counting on it. There's no place on earth for him other than the pit of hell!"

— *Felicia Sanders*

But Judge Gergel stated that he believed her testimony was an interpretation of her religious belief and it was a religious comment. He also instructed the jury that any decision on guilt or a sentence would be totally up to the jury and not the attorneys or witnesses for the case.

Dylann Roof's trial was the second highest profile trial ever to take place in Charleston. The other was the murder of a black man by a former North Charleston police officer, Michael Slager, who shot and killed a black motorist, Walter Scott, in April 2015. Although his case ended in a hung jury, Dylann Roof would not be so lucky. The highlight of the trial would be Dylann Roof himself who would confess to the FBI that he committed the heinous crime while being recorded. He laid out detailed information about how and why he did it. "He pulled the trigger more than 70 times that night. More than 60 times he hit parishioners," Assistant U.S. Attorney Jay

Richardson told jurors as a part of his opening statement.

"He seemed to be harmless to them. Little did they know what a cold and hateful heart he had."
— *Attorney Jay Richardson*

WHAT IS LOOKED UPON AS AN AMERICAN DREAM FOR WHITE PEOPLE HAS LONG BEEN AN AMERICAN NIGHTMARE FOR BLACK PEOPLE.
— *Malcolm X*
New York City
May 1, 1962

BORN

TO

KILL

Chapter One

Young Dylann

Roof was born on April 3, 1994 in Columbia, South Carolina. His father, Franklin Bennett Roof was an ordinary man, a carpenter and a construction contractor. His mother, Amelia "Amy" Cowles, was a bartender and a descendant of Hartford, Connecticut's founder Timothy Stanley. He had always been a strange kid but no one really took notice. Before his birth, his parents had already filed for divorce but decided to give their marriage another try when young Dylann was born. But it didn't last long. By the time Dylann was five his father had fallen in love with another woman and decided to marry Paige Mann in November of 1999. Things would be good and Dylann accepted his stepmother and even came to love her after feeling neglected by his real mother.

But Dylann would have his heart ripped out of him again when after 10 years his father filed for divorce. It was rumored that his father was abusive, verbally and physically, toward the woman Dylann knew as his mother. When his stepmother and father separated, he took it hard. They moved around, making it hard for Dylann to ever truly develop a real friendship with anyone and it was later reported in 2009 he exhibited "obsessive compulsive behavior" while growing up. He would obsess over germs and was adamant about how he wanted his hair cut. He knew he was different but didn't shy away from it or try to hide it. He also took up an interest in drugs (as most teenagers do) and was once caught trying to purchase some marijuana.

He wasn't a stable kid and ended up attending seven schools in a period of nine years, all in various counties throughout South Carolina. He attended White Knoll High School in Lexington where he was forced to repeat the ninth grade in another school. He would eventually become frustrated; feeling like school wasn't doing anything for him. So in 2010, he made a decision to quit school altogether. Roof just dropped out of school with no serious plan for the future. He had no idea what he wanted to become or what he wanted to do. According to family members, poor Dylann just wanted to play video games and do drugs. His favorite drug was Suboxone. But he also took an interest in a local Evangelical Lutheran congregation. He began to do a lot of drinking, he continued doing drugs and lived back and forth with his father and stepmother, Paige Mann, whom he still loved. He would also live-in with a friend he knew from middle school who lived with his mother, his friends, two brothers and a girlfriend. Needless to say, it was obvious that the house was crowded.

Poor Dylann had no purpose in life and no real home. His father was disappointed in his decisions. He got him a job doing landscaping but Dylann would quit like he did everything else. He was actually homeless and a drifter who lived off other people for free. His uncle, Carson Cowles, the brother of his biological mother, had expressed concerns to her about his nephew and his withdrawal from social interactions when Dylan was once living with him. He told her, "Dylan didn't have a job, a driver's license or anything like that. He just stayed in his room a lot of the time." Dylann felt like no one understood him. Therefore, he decided his company was his best company. His uncle made attempts to mentor him but was rejected and it caused their relationship to become strained. Dylan drifted further and further away from his uncle. And although he loved his mother, he secretly blamed her for leaving him so he cut her out of his life. He did the same with his sister, including not responding to her wedding invitation. He became a loner and began to form a hatred for people, especially blacks.

"Despite his racist comments, some of his friends in school were black."
— *Classmate*

But having a black friend didn't mean shit to Dylann. Sometimes even racist people will start to like a black person if he actually gives himself a chance to know them. Plus, although Dylann might have been born racist, he didn't realize it until later in life, unless he was keeping it to himself. It was obvious Roof had a serious problem with black people. It didn't matter if he had a black friend or not. Maybe it was all just a façade; maybe it was just an act. But once he became triggered, there was no turning back. Roof would eventually become obsessed with the hatred he had for black people.

And if he did have black friends, they're lucky to be alive.

Run-Ins

Although he wasn't a hard-core criminal he did have run-ins with the police. There was a prior police record for two arrests, both in a few months before the attack. Dylann was in a mall at the Columbiana Centre in Columbia, South Carolina where he was involved in an incident on February 28, 2015. He was dressed in all-black clothing and began to aggressively ask employees in the mall unsettling questions. A complaint was made with the police who finally caught up with him on March 2, 2015. During questioning, officers noticed and confiscated a bottle, which Dylann admitted, contained Suboxone. It's a narcotic used for either treating opiate addictions or is sometimes used as a recreational drug.

Officers arrested Roof and charged him with a misdemeanor for drug possession. He was banned from the Columbiana Centre for a year as punishment, but that didn't stop Dylann. He trespassed and violated the sanction on April 26th when he entered the mall again. After being caught, the ban was extended for an additional three years. Per the office of the former FBI Director, James Comey, Roof's March arrest was at first written as a felony which if it hadn't been changed, would have generated a mandatory inquiry into the charge during a firearms background check on him. And the former FBI head agrees it was first written incorrectly and that legally it was always supposed to be a misdemeanor. It was reported that it was the jail clerk whose entry into the database was wrong. Had it stayed as it was first written, Roof would not have been able to legally enter a gun store and purchase a gun under the law which bars "unlawful users of (or addicted to) any type of controlled substance" from owning a firearm.

After his first arrest it wouldn't take long for Roof to find himself in trouble with the law again. It was becoming clear that Roof had chosen a life of crime but no one could have ever believed how far he would go. Eleven days after being questioned and then busted by officers for drugs, he would be investigated for loitering. They found him in his parked car not far from a park in downtown Columbia. He was spotted and recognized by one of the officers who questioned him in the March 2nd incident. He called in for backup and conducted a search of Roof's vehicle. During the search the officers found a forearm grip for an AR-15 semiautomatic rifle and six unloaded magazine clips with the capability of holding 40 rounds.

"Wow, Roof. What are you planning on shooting?" an officer asked after discovering the gun paraphernalia.

"I just wanted to purchase an AR-15 but I didn't have enough money to do so," he explained.

Since it was not illegal to possess a firearm grip in South Carolina, Dylann Roof was not charged and let go.

Chapter Two

Attention

Dylann Roof was tired of being a "nobody." He had been invisible all his life as if he was never there. He had no voice. When he talked nobody listened which is probably why when he did tell a few people things nobody took him seriously. He was fed up with not being heard; with not being taken seriously; and with being a nobody. He wanted attention. He yearned for it. He wanted respect, something he'd never had, and when he talked he wanted people to listen. Dylann wanted what everybody else had and to do that he had to find a way to court attention at all cost.

Everything is judged by its appearance; what is not seen counts for nothing; what is never heard counts for nothing; you never allow yourself to be lost in the crowd or even worse, to be buried into oblivion. These were the mantras Roof would begin to live by. He realized if he wanted to change how people perceived him, he would have to find a way to "stand out." He had to become conspicuous at all costs, no matter the consequences. He had to make himself a magnet to draw attention. He needed to appear larger than what he was which is what he had always wanted to be. Roof wanted his name to be talked about in everyone's mouth — from people who knew him and from people who didn't. He wanted the media to talk about him or maybe write a book about him or even possibly make a movie about him. He felt he needed to be more mysterious, which wasn't hard for him because he was already very mysterious. He was a very timid man (or child) and he knew he needed to be bold.

But Dylann Roof was destined to draw attention to himself even becoming obsessed with doing so. He had a strong desire to create an unforgettable and controversial image. He knew people always paid close attention to controversy. "With what I'm about to do, the world will never forget me," he mumbled to himself. He was ready to do anything that could make him the center of attention. It was his destiny to shine more brightly than those around him. He had a desire to prove to himself that he was not just ordinary but instead extraordinary. He had come to the conclusion that any kind of attention would be good even if it was considered bad to some people. And he was right. Making no distinction between the kinds of attention/notoriety that will come will bring any man power. As far as Dylan Roof believed, "It was better to be slandered and attacked than to be ignored."

It was something Roof was born with. He didn't know how to burn more brighter than those around him. But he noticed once he started acting like a racist, white supremacists started paying attention to him. He started to get noticed and people began caring about what poor Dylan had to say. Therefore, this was something he had to learn. He felt that if he ever wanted to be respected he had to be willing to do what others wouldn't do. He had to see and separate himself from the ordinary racists who only talked the talk but didn't walk the walk. He already had a look which was unique so he was halfway there. He was standoffish and considered weird, therefore any kind of drastic act would catapult him into the public. It is believed Roof stumbled upon his mission to commit mass murder. It was like once he got a taste of receiving attention, there was no limit for him. Dylann Roof would do whatever it took to court attention at all cost.

"Court attention at all cost."

— *Robert Greene*

Art of Timing

Dylann Roof imagined he could start a war between blacks and whites. He believed that with all the police shootings of blacks, especially the one committed by Michael Slager, he believed the war had already started and he would be the one to take it to another level. Racial tension was already high in America during 2014 and 2015. Therefore, it was the perfect time to ignite a race war. Blacks were mad about the laws surrounding mass incarceration of their people which resulted in ripping away primarily black father's from their families, leaving their children fatherless. It was a calculated form of high-tech slavery where the men would be in prison for a minimum of 10 years to life and would be forced to work in prison factories for 6¢ per hour. All the laws in the U.S. are designed to lock blacks up forever — and it seemed to be working.

The "three strikes" law and its enhancements are the most diabolical laws ever made known to man. Crimes committed by whites received much lower sentences to be served at 50% which meant they only served half their time, sometimes only 33%, whereas blacks served 85% with much longer sentences. So Dylann was banking on that for himself. He was banking on the art of timing. With all the shootings and the presidential race with Donald Trump, the whites and blacks were expressing their true feelings. He had waited long enough. He'd kept his hatred inside himself too long and it was bottled up and ready to burst out. He had become a detective of the "right moment" and could sniff out the spirit of the times. He knew that what he wanted to do would give him the power he'd dreamed of and felt he finally deserved. He had stood in the background too long because he knew the time wasn't right. But now he was ready to strike and strike fiercely! His dream of killing blacks had reached its fruition and he was ready to make it his reality. But Roof didn't want to appear in a hurry. He didn't run around telling all of his white supremacist brothers. It was like he knew that to be in a hurry would have proved his lack of control. Instead, although it did materialize within months after the sudden urge for Roof to become a radical racist, it didn't appear as if he was in a hurry.

Roof appeared patient until he received enough money to purchase the weapon needed. Yet he was still indecisive on how or where he would commit his vicious act. It was like he knew that in time everything would eventually come together; all of his unanswered questions would be answered: How would it come full circle? How would he be remembered? Was he truly the chosen one? But it was clear to him that the actions of the past plus the actions of today made it ripe for his horrific act to be carried out. Roof seemed to become hateful overnight; a hate so vicious it was not just a passing thought but may have started out as small as a mustard seed and grew into the act of mass murder it became. It was apparent that when Roof got an idea into his head he would act on it. He became obsessed with it and slowly but surely allowed it to materialize into something real, so much so that Dylan Roof began making plans to show just how real it was to him.

About The Author

My aspirations and achievements were born out of great sacrifice, including being buried alive (by incarceration). My writing is an authentic gift which transports me into other worlds; some I create and others I learn about. It's extremely educational, especially when it comes to the history of our country. It's an eye-opener, an experience that's unexplainable and a very emotional ride. I've done music, videos and mini-movies but writing captures me; it engulfs me. It allows vision and escape from my pain and reality. I want others to see what I've realized.

Feel free to send any comments (positive or negative) you may have about my books. Although I write out of passion, I also write for you (my readers). Insight and knowledge is power. I hope to become the engineer of the human soul. It is with books, as with men, a very small number will play a great part. I'm striving to be one of those men. Send comments to:

Mr. Genaro Patterson

#AR7758

CHCF

7707 South Austin Road

Stockton, CA 95213

genaro.patterson.hfo@gmail.com